# After the Purple Heart

a novel

JAMES RANDALL MILLER

Based on a previously published book, *Far From Eden,* by James Randall Miller.

Biblical quotations used in this book are from the *World English Bible,* located online at: http://ebible.org/web.

Peace Pilgrim quotations used in this book are from www.peacepilgrim.org.

Lao Tzu quotations used in this book are from the 1996 English translation of the *Tao Te Ching* by J. H. McDonald, located online at: http://www.wright-house.com/religions/taoism/tao-te-ching

Inquiries should be addressed to the author at: jamesmillerbooks@gmail.com

Printed in the United States of America

ISBN-13: 978-0-9834150-3-9 (paperback)

ISBN-13: 978-0-9834150-4-6 (eBook)

# DEDICATION

*For David, my brother,*
*who passed away all too soon,*
*and Allen, my father.*
*May you rest in eternal peace.*

*And my deep gratitude to the sages in this book*
*and to all those who have guided me*
*along the course of my journey...*

*"It is such a secret place, the land of tears."*
– Antoine de Saint-Exupéry

*"I shut my eyes in order to see."*
– Paul Gauguin

# PART ONE

*endings and beginnings*

# 1

*Taji, Iraq*

AFTER PULLING INTO a former school playground, First Lieutenant Jon David Luke exited his armored Humvee, took a long swig from his water bottle, and eyed with a frown the early morning sun.

"Jesus," he muttered. "Jesus, Jesus, Jesus." He tossed the container back into the Humvee and paused to adjust his Improved Outer Tactical Vest, a fancy name for body armor. Beads of sweat, muddy with the ever-present fine desert dust, streamed down his forehead in response to the unrelenting sun. Cursing the morning temperature was premature. The predicted 115-degree afternoon heat would soon make this time seem cool. After eighty-three days on the line, without thinking, he checked the safety of his M4 assault rifle, tightened the strap of his Kevlar helmet, and readjusted his impact-resistant sunglasses. He took a long breath, cursed the weight of his gear for the thousandth time since beginning this tour, and went to the senior noncommissioned officer.

"Never in my four years at West Point and Ranger school did I think I'd be doing this kind of soldiering." His remark drew a smirk from the sergeant.

"You want a stick of Big Red?" The offer of gum was silently accepted.

With that, Jon David Luke spoke in a voice loud enough for all to hear. "Sergeant Frisby, gather the men." The NCO summoned the soldiers with a simple arm gesture.

The fifteen-man squad and their Iraqi interpreter assembled around the lieutenant, knowing his patrols always began with a perfunctory pep talk. One private called it the military version of the Wal-Mart cheer, only the stakes in this job were a little higher than working at a big-box store. A mistake here might result in a trip home in a box. The lieutenant's straightforward spiel consisted of three rules, and demanded total participation.

"Rule one!" he boomed.

"Stay together!" the men shouted back with enthusiasm.

"An American soldier is a propaganda bonanza to the insurgents. They want nothing more than to broadcast you being separated from your head... Rule two!"

"Vigilance!"

"You start daydreaming, your ass is as good as dead."

He eyed every one of them.

"Rule three!"

"Don't die!" All the men hoped they wouldn't let their leader down regarding rule number three.

Jon David paused, bowed his head, and spoke in a humble tone. "Sweet Jesus, please bless us with your divine protection." The group stood reverently for a few moments. The lieutenant broke the silence. "All right, cowboys, I expect no rectal-cranial inversion today. In other words, keep your head out of your ass."

"Hooah!"

The men returned to their four Humvees for the rest of their gear. Given the heat, some gulped down more water while others loaded up with a fresh can of Skoal. Since smoking was banned on combat patrols, chewing tobacco became a must-have item for many who needed to appease their nicotine habit. Within a couple of minutes, the squad was ready.

"Hey, everyone—one last thing!" boomed Jon David. "Mr. Al-Jamil informs me that Islam forbids putting your forehead on the ground except in prayer, and there's no greater humiliation than forcing a man's head down. Keep that in mind when we do house-to-house weapon searches today. If we subdue someone, it will be done with reasonable restraint and with respect to their customs and courtesies."

Haakim Al-Jamil, the squad's Iraqi interpreter, nodded in an animated way to emphasize the point. In this turbulent land, Haakim had become Jon David's trusted friend. The short, paunchy, mustachioed, mid-thirties former school teacher was the physical antithesis of the tall, ramrod straight, steely-eyed lieutenant with hard and chiseled features. The dissimilarities didn't end there. While Jon David carried himself with an easy, confident style that some said bordered on arrogance, Haakim was quiet and studious, with an abundance of patience to tolerate this brash American who went by the Hollywood nickname "Cool Hand Luke." Yet despite their differences, the two spent many hours together. Haakim taught him about Islam and its cherished traditions; the lieutenant schooled him in the nuances of American language, including choice pick-up lines for the ladies.

Jon David eyed the sun again and shook his head. "Make sure you all have enough water. Let's move out." He began moving to the north side of the hard-packed dirt road and swiveled around to face his men. "Everyone stay wicked sharp!"

With him on point, they slowly moved up the narrow sidewalk, toward the shop-lined streets at the center of town. The squad's four Humvees, each with a driver and gunner, followed seventy-five feet behind. The gunners stood in the vehicles, ready to provide suppressive fire with Browning .50-caliber M2 "Ma-deuce" machine guns mounted on the roof turrets.

Today's mission called for patrolling the streets of Taji to keep order by suppressing terrorist and criminal activity. Subordinate to this came exploring ways with the local tribal leaders to improve civil services and infrastructure. This would be a huge feat. Most of the town's buildings were spattered with bullet holes from recent and bygone skirmishes. The roads fared no better, being pockmarked from detonated improvised explosive devices. This once-thriving village looked like a place on the outskirts of hell.

A noxious mélange of odors wafted up from the open gutters lining the road. Trash bags, tossed in the street, appeared to be breeding, bearing testament to a sporadic-at-best garbage removal service. An occasional dead dog added to the insufferable stench. The lieutenant scanned the sidewalk and street—the trash, the dead dogs, any fresh digging in the street—all were perfect places for hiding explosives.

The townspeople scurried about, many heading to the markets early to beat the heat of the day. With irregular electricity and blistering temperatures, perishable food items had to be bought and quickly consumed. In the by-gone days of working refrigerators, once a week food shopping trips could sustain a family; the new reality required daily visits to the market. This increased the number of people on the streets, which gave terrorists/insurgents two distinct advantages—an abundance of targets and the ability to quickly disappear into the crowd.

Relations between Americans and Iraqis were tenuous at best. Some locals barely contained their hatred of "the invaders." Evidence of this came with either guarded glances or menacing stares from men, and averted eye contact from women, many of whom were dressed in the traditional black hijab. Children, on the other hand, were a different story. They swarmed around the soldiers, especially their tall leader. Jon David was a natural born kid-magnet. They loved his easy smile and the big, lung-busting hugs he dispensed. He learned several of their names—Haady, Badar, Na'eem, Pir, Ja'far, and Aban. Each day brought new names to be remembered. In the course of this tour, he gave out so many sticks of Big Red that he had to draft his mom in Virginia to ship a couple of cases to him each month.

Despite the friendly street urchins, there was business to tend to. Taji remained a dangerous place. Jon David's finger never moved far from the trigger of his M4 assault rifle, and his eyes constantly scanned the crowd. His soldiers followed suit, each looking for anything suspicious. Awareness and the ability to respond quickly meant life.

The country's porous borders presented an open-door invitation for foreign Sunni Muslim extremists, known in Army parlance as Al-Qaida in Iraq, or AQI. The morning's intelligence briefing warned of roving bands of them potentially traversing the area after being routed from Fallujah. Jon David bristled at the thought of these armed thugs who had a penchant for capturing American soldiers and civilians for internet-broadcast beheadings. The shock-factor of this was far higher than improvised explosive devices, which they used to ambush military convoys. Lieutenant Luke had no qualms about dispatching these sinister people.

Twenty feet ahead, a nervous-looking man abruptly crossed the street when the Americans appeared. Lieutenant Luke noticed and motioned with a pointed finger for privates Scudder and Goodwin to intercept him. The soldiers stopped the man and patted him down for weapons. Private Scudder looked at Jon David and shook his head, indicating he was unarmed. Jon David, Haakim, and Sergeant Frisby moved to the sweating Iraqi, who appeared to be in his early twenties.

"Ask him why he is so nervous."

"He says his father has been taken to the hospital with chest pains, and he is hurrying to go there."

"What is his dad's name?"

"Ahmed Yasim Gumar."

Jon David's eyes bore into the brown eyes of the nervous Iraqi. He had a knack of knowing when someone was lying. Darting eyes were a dead giveaway. A few moments passed with no words being spoken. "Tell him I hope Allah is merciful to his father." After Haakim did the translating, the face of the man seemed to lighten with relief. He nodded and went on his way.

"Sergeant Frisby, let's split up the men to cover both sides of the street. Haakim, I want to drop in on Mr. Khalaf today and maybe Mr. Al-Robaei, if we have time." Khalaf and Al-Robaei were two of the local tribal leaders.

Haakim raised an eyebrow. "Mr. Khalaf?"

"Yeah. He's as slippery as a snake in wet grass, but I think he's starting to succumb to my charms."

"I believe you are right about him being a snake. Be very careful, Jon David. Whoever pats scorpions with the hand of compassion gets stung." Jon David laughed at the remark. Although he agreed with Haakim, like it or not, peace in Taji was necessarily linked to Abdul Khalaf and the other tribal leaders.

Mr. Khalaf owned a tobacco shop a couple of blocks down the road. Jon David always suspected it was little more than a front for black market activities that were making Abdul wealthy. He frowned at the thought of this man profiting off the misery of others. On the bright side, discussions with the other leaders were producing measured cooperation. True negotiations, Jon David learned, only occur when sitting in one of their homes or shops swilling multiple cups of traditional chai, the Iraqi version of tea. Haakim's advice always played in his head: *"My friend, if you listen, you have the advantage; if you speak, others have it."* In this culture, proper deference was the key to cooperation. If kowtowing kept his men alive, Jon David was more than willing to have one of the brownest noses in the United States Army. The art— the delicate balance—focused on mutual respect. Conceding too much was a sign of weakness; being a tyrant could result in an insurrection.

As the days went by, the village leaders found Lieutenant Luke to be a strong and determined leader with the confidence of a lion. Though half their age, this young officer was not a man to cross. Although still suspicious of American intentions, they came to see him as a fair man who cared about their wellbeing. He won their respect for listening to their constant railings about no electricity, long gas lines, lack of jobs, and a hundred other ills. Occasionally, Jon David would pull off a minor miracle, such as when he brought in a gas-powered generator to keep the hospital lights on. Money for rebuilding the local school also elevated his standing with the locals. His love of their children did not pass unnoticed by even the most hardened of hearts. Slowly, the residents of Taji began to accept Jon David Luke as "their" lieutenant.

The soldiers turned left at the intersection of the main street. The sidewalks were wider, giving them more room to move among the people. The sun approached its zenith, which sent the temperature skyrocketing to 115 degrees. Jon David remembered his youth, growing up in the Roanoke Valley of Virginia. Summers meant biking on the Blue Ridge Parkway or water sports at Smith Mountain Lake. This hot and dusty place made him ever more appreciative of the land that he called home.

Ten minutes up the road brought Jon David and his squad to Mr. Khalaf's tobacco shop. He motioned them to hold up while he and Haakim went inside to pay their respects. To his surprise, Mr. Khalaf was nowhere to be seen, which was quite unusual since the man practically lived at the store.

"Where is Mr. Khalaf?" Haakim asked a pimple-faced teenager minding the shop. A shrug of the shoulders was the reply. Jon David nodded, turned, and proceeded with Haakim back to the street where the ever-present kids waited. The squad moved forward another ten meters. Jon David stopped and looked in a pottery shop. The owner greeted him with a slight smile. He decided to go in and motioned for Haakim to follow. He surveyed the room, which was outfitted with an ad hoc assortment of differently painted wooden shelves and a dust-covered kiln in the rear. A sweet and pungent odor from burning incense permeated the space. The pottery resting on the pathetic shelves was exquisite, consisting of finely crafted yellow clay bowls with opaque glazes. He was fascinated by the quality and craftsmanship of the work. Through Haakim, he asked the potter about his glazing technique. The man beamed at the attention and replied that the glaze turns opaque after firing, creating what he called "pearl cups like the moon."

Lieutenant Luke looked the potter straight in the eye. "Please tell this man he is a master," he said to Haakim. After the words were said, Jon David bowed to the delighted man, shook his hand, and exited the shop.

Back on the street, he glanced at his watch. They needed to pick up the pace to keep the mission within its planned time parameters. He looked at Sergeant Frisby and saw the sergeant nod, silently seconding the lieutenant's notion. *Yes, my vigilant sergeant, I will hurry,* he thought to himself, unable to hide a smile. He headed up the street with a gaggle of Iraqi boys in tow.

Near an intersecting road about twenty meters ahead, the lieutenant noticed some fast-moving men. This flutter of activity was followed by the shrill screams of women who began scrambling away from them. Suddenly, a man wielding a long tube jumped out from behind a van stopped at the intersection.

"*RPG! RPG!*" Jon David screamed, warning of a rocket propelled grenade. Before he could move his M4 rifle, the man, dressed in traditional Arab clothing, launched the grenade. Jon David saw a puff of smoke, heard the recognizable pop, and saw the big grenade ball exit the tube. It whooshed by him and made a beeline for the first Humvee. *Boom!* The RPG obliterated the driver's armored windshield and exploded inside, sending a fireball into the air through the vehicle's roof turret. The driver and gunner died instantly.

Jon David whipped up his rifle, took quick aim, and fired a three-bullet semi-automatic burst. The bullets found the shooter's chest. He crumpled to the ground. More insurgents piled out of two parked vans, carrying an assortment of RPGs and AK-47 Kalashnikov automatic rifles. Still on point and a good three meters from Sergeant Frisby, Jon David had the best angle for taking them out. He screamed at the kids to get down, but they were frozen in place, looking like wide-eyed little statues. Pandemonium filled the street—screaming residents dashed about in search of cover; some dove into shop entrances while others dropped to the ground. One woman stopped in the middle of the road, intent on picking up several oranges that tumbled from her shopping bag, testimony to how panic affects people in peculiar ways.

He squeezed off another burst, hitting an insurgent in the leg. The man dropped to the ground and crawled to the safety of a parked car. The muzzle flash from Jon David's rifle caught the eye of another insurgent toting an RPG. He aimed the rocket and fired. *Whoosh! Boom!* The grenade hit a two-story stone-walled building behind Jon David and exploded. The entire wall came crashing down, annihilating the group of children, and slamming him to the ground. The blast jettisoned his M4, propelling it into the street. Momentarily stunned, he shook off the stars dancing in his vision, and willed his eyes to resume seeing.

An Iraqi boy, Haady, lay next to him, mouth open, with lifeless eyes staring directly at him. Jon David gasped and recoiled. Dust and smoke filled the air, mixed with the concentrated stench of cordite. Blood oozed from his ears, no doubt the consequence of burst eardrums. Intense stinging pain came from every part of his body not covered by ballistic protection. He reached for his M9 Beretta as Sergeant Frisby rushed forward and helped him to his feet.

"Where's Haakim?" Jon David shouted.

"Dead!" He pointed to his crushed body near the side of the wall.

"Get the Ma-deuces focused on the vans!" The sergeant nodded and ran toward the Humvees. An AK-47 round caught him in the neck, dropping him in his tracks. He gasped for breath. Blood poured from his mouth. His death came quickly.

Jon David let out a howl of anger. He hoisted the sergeant to his shoulder and began running back to his men. A bullet slammed into his left arm, spinning him around, causing him to lose his balance. He fell hard yet again and felt something snap in his jaw when his face hit the ground. Another RPG whooshed by, barely missing the second Humvee. Its gunner was sweeping the streets with the Browning. Chunks of stone were flying off the buildings, and huge dirt divots flew up from the street as each punishing round from the machine gun hit anything solid.

With Sergeant Frisby gone, Jon David was fifteen meters from the nearest squad members, who were drifting back to the relative safety of the Humvees. *Not good, not good,* he thought as he lay on the ground. The fall interrupted his view of the enemy. He swiveled around and gasped—at least eight insurgents were rushing his way. They crouched as they ran, taking advantage of the parked cars to shield them from the Humvee gunners. Jon David shot the pack's leader with his Beretta, and then the one behind him. The others ducked behind cars for cover. He leaped up and grabbed the lifeless body of Sergeant Frisby—none of his men would be left behind. An insurgent jumped out and rolled a grenade down the sidewalk, tossing it underhanded, like a bowling ball. The grenade skipped along until it got to within two feet of Jon David's left leg. *Boom!* The grenade exploded in a thunderous roar, sending chards of shrapnel and hot gas flying. His body cartwheeled. He landed hard on his left shoulder.

Jon David screamed in pain from the blazing hot metal chunks perforating his body. *Oh Jesus! Oh Jesus!* He looked down and was horrified to see the shiny white bones of his left leg sticking out at grotesque angles through his scorched uniform, along with pulsing jets of blood shooting into the air. He tried to reach for his leg to stop the blood, but his left arm wouldn't move. *Oh Jesus!* He fought the urge to panic. *Get back to the men! Oh Jesus!*

His eye caught movement. The insurgent who rolled the grenade was running toward him. *Shoot him!* his mind demanded. He fired his Beretta multiple times. The man dropped two feet away from his bleeding legs. Jon David crawled to a shop doorway with all his remaining strength. Nausea and light-headedness swept over him. His vision turned hazy.

The insurgents now focused on the wounded American like a flock of hungry vultures. "Don't shoot him!" one screamed in Arabic. "Get him! Get him!" Three of them sprinted to him without firing their weapons. This prize warranted a little recklessness.

Jon David saw them. There weren't enough bullets remaining in his clip to kill all of them. *This is it, they got you. Shoot yourself!* He struggled to move his pistol to his head. Suddenly, a loud blast rang out from the doorway behind him. The three insurgents dropped in unison, riddled with bullets from an AK-47. Jon David looked around and saw the potter he met earlier. "Not worry, Lieutenant, I take care you!" He tossed his weapon down and grabbed Jon David by the collar, pulling him into his shop. It was the last thing the lieutenant would ever hear in Taji, succumbing at that moment to the ether of unconsciousness.

The potter yanked an extension cord from an outlet and tightly wrapped it around the lieutenant's left leg just below the knee. He grabbed Jon David by the collar again and pulled him out the back doorway and into the alley. He struggled to get the unconscious man into the back seat of his battered Toyota, and then jumped into the driver's seat. Hands trembling, he put the key into the ignition and prayed the car would start on the first try. *"Inshah Allah! Inshah Allah! Inshah Allah!"* he said, which in Arabic means *by the will of God*. The engine sputtered to life and the potter jammed the accelerator to the floorboard.

The car surged forward, its tires squealing. An insurgent dashed out and fired a wild burst from his AK-47 at the car. A fusillade of lead shattered the back window. The potter felt a bullet whiz by his ear and through the front glass. He made an abrupt, tire-squealing turn at an intersecting road to avoid the hail of gunfire. "Not worry, Lieutenant, not worry," he said again, "I take care you, I take care you!" He sped to the one place he knew offered safety—the American's base.

The soldiers manning the Camp Taji gate heard the gunfire coming from the town. They knew Lt. Luke's patrol was likely taking fire. Two kilometers down the road, an old civilian car came racing toward them. "Heads up!" shouted a private. Everyone leveled their weapons at the vehicle bearing down on them at great speed. A soldier raised his arms and waved, motioning the car to stop. The vehicle screeched to a zigzagging halt and the occupant jumped out of the driver's side door. He raced to soldiers, flailing his arms like a madman. The lead sergeant wasted no time. *"Fire!"* He pulled the trigger of his M249 Squad Automatic Weapon Light Machine Gun. Bullets from his weapon and a multitude of others found their mark. The potter landed with a thud on the pavement, eyes open and staring into space. He was dead before he hit the ground.

The car's engine was still running as it was approached by the wary soldiers. "My God!" yelled a private. "There's someone in uniform in the back seat." He moved closer and recognized the Army Combat Uniform. "It's an ACU! An ACU!" The lead sergeant muscled his way in. "Christ, it's an officer!" he shouted upon seeing a black lieutenant insignia on the man's uniform. He then saw the name sewn on a patch—LUKE. "It's Cool Hand Luke! He's hurt bad. Call the medics, quick, damn it."

The medics did their best to stabilize the critically injured lieutenant. A UH-60Q Black Hawk helicopter arrived within minutes and he was quickly loaded into its cavity. With a swift upward jerk on the collective, the pilot sent the helicopter leaping into the air and vectored it to a nearby theater hospital. Jon David had sixteen minutes remaining on his "golden hour"—military jargon for the hour immediately following major trauma, where prompt medical care is critical to the injured person's survival.

# 2

JON DAVID RALLIED, and willed his mind to limited awareness.

*"What...the...hell?"* he mouthed. With great effort, he opened his eyes. Intense, bright light assaulted his vision, forcing his eyes to shut. It felt like he was lying on some sort of vibrating contraption until he realized his body was violently shivering. *Why am I cold when it's 115 degrees?* he wondered. He heard voices nearby and strained to discern what they were saying.

"Damn, what to tackle first?" one said, followed by a more authoritative, "Okay, people, give me the rundown, item-by-item from the top." Then came a hesitant response: "Frag in the face, eyewear saved his eyes, soft tissue mouth trauma, possible jaw fracture, perforated ear drums, possible concussion, dislocated left shoulder, broken collarbone, significant arm lacerations, bullet wound in the left bicep, likely wrist fracture." A pause. "Severe lacerations to the left leg below the knee, fractured tibia and fibula; more lacerations on the right leg, possible gunshot in the thigh, second degree burns on both legs." The medic was being kind in describing the left leg. It was a crushed and shrapnel-mangled mess. The authoritative voice spoke again. "Get me another two units of O positive. Put out the word that we'll need at least ten more units."

*"Where...am...I?"* Lieutenant Luke weakly asked. The words were hard to form and his voice didn't sound right to him. He felt lumps in his mouth and spit them out. Two teeth, mixed with blood and a bit of tissue. A metallic taste filled his mouth. He knew the taste; he remembered it from his teenage days playing football. It was blood. He fought the urge to gag.

"Easy, Lieutenant," said a soft female voice. "I'm a nurse. You've been wounded and have been airlifted to a theater hospital. I promise we'll take great care of you."

Jon David labored to hear her over the loud gushing noises in both of his ears. He tried to reach out and pull her closer. "I c-c-can't s-stop sh-sh-shivering," he struggled to say, but his words were near unintelligible. "C-c-cold. Men, m-m-my men?"

The soft, comforting voice spoke again. "You've lost a lot of blood and it's lowered your body temperature. That's why you're shivering."

More voices filled the room, but Jon David couldn't make his mind understand what they were saying. Then the soft voice spoke again, this time close to his ear. He could feel her breath on his face. "We're going to give you some medication and you'll soon drift off. I'll be praying for you." Within moments his thoughts drifted to nothingness…

The medical events that would take place in the next forty-eight hours to save the young lieutenant's life were nothing short of extraordinary. Fifteen minutes after arriving at the theater hospital, Jon David was whisked to an operating room, located inside an austere-looking refrigerated metal trailer. The exterior of the theater operating room belied the medical marvels within. Any big-city ER staff would drool at the array of medical devices crammed into the room. A team of doctors descended upon the limp lieutenant. The anesthesiologist claimed his turf near Jon David's head. A maxillofacial surgeon eyed a fresh set of x-rays. First dibs on the surgical instruments went to the orthopedic surgeon, who surveyed the nearly severed leg. His diagnosis was swift.

"Let's amputate it."

The nursing team hit the afterburner with those words, scurrying about for the specialized equipment the surgeon would need.

"Ligature." A nurse handed him a device he expertly used to tie off the supplying arteries and veins to prevent further hemorrhage. "That cord saved his life," he said to no one in particular. "Let's remove it now." He paused while a nurse cut and removed the improvised tourniquet. With a scalpel, he transected muscles and ligaments. Cauterized blood vessels filled the room with the acrid odor of burning flesh. He then sawed through the bones with an oscillating saw, followed by transposing skin and muscle flaps over the stump. Then came the sewing, packing, and bandaging. The entire procedure was swift. Sadly, this skilled surgeon had plenty of practice. Focus shifted to the other leg. As he tossed pieces of razor-sharp, twisted RPG and hand grenade shrapnel into a metal container, they made a distinct, ringing noise. The stone wall fragments extracted from the lieutenant's flesh made more of a thudding sound when they hit the bin. Finally, the surgeon looked at the rest of the team. A slight nod indicated he was through. The rest of his colleagues then took their respective turns. Jon David was on the operating table several hours that day.

Six hours after exiting the operating room, another Black Hawk medivac transported Lieutenant Luke to Joint Base Balad, about sixty-eight kilometers north of Baghdad. There, he and other wounded soldiers were prepped for an aeromedical evacuation aboard a specially equipped C-17 aircraft. A flight surgeon, specializing in flight physiology, had to clear them for travel, as changes in altitude can adversely alter a patient's stability.

Another team of medical technicians aboard the C-17 would accompany the wounded. Jon David never knew that an attractive ER-trained female doctor watched him like a hawk for the entire five-hour flight to Ramstein Air Force Base in Germany. From there came a quick ten-minute ride by bus to the Army's Landstuhl Regional Medical Center.

Jon David awoke the following day, racked with every conceivable kind of acute pain imaginable—throbbing, dull, aching, ice-pick sharp—and it seemed to be emanating from everywhere at once. He fought to keep from crying out. A tired looking man walked in and halfheartedly smiled.

"Hello, Lieutenant Luke, my name is Chaplain Greer. I'm afraid I have some bad news to share with you. I'll get right to the point. You've suffered significant injuries, the most appreciable one being the amputation of your leg below the knee. The docs will explain the rest of your injuries when you are feeling better. I, uh, I have an initial situation report regarding your squad. I'm sorry, but four of your men did not survive, and three others were wounded, one severely. That's all I know about what happened, but rest assured, those wounded are receiving the finest of care." He pointed to a Purple Heart medal pinned to Jon David's pillow. "You earned this. Our country is indebted to you." He looked at his watch and frowned. "I have to go. There's another case requiring my presence. I'll drop by later and see how you're doing." He touched Jon David's hand, offered a sad smile, and left.

Tears trickled down Lieutenant Luke's swollen face, rehydrating some of the dried blood still there from the battle. His mind repeated what the chaplain had said. *You lost four of your men.* With this realization, the slow trail of tears turned into torrents from his weeping. On this day in a busy hospital in Germany, Jon David Luke, like Icarus of Greek mythology, began a downward spiral, heading for an abrupt rendezvous with the unrelenting earth.

# 3

*Three days later…*

EERILY FAMILIAR VOICES filled the room, but they were too quiet to hear. It was the tones and inflections that he was sure he'd heard before. Jon David thought about the sounds some more before drifting back into a drug-induced haze. An hour later, throbbing pain returned him to semi consciousness. The voices were still there. He felt a cool washcloth touching his forehead. Suddenly, fierce stabbing pains acting like smelling salts slammed him into full consciousness. He screamed out in pain as his eyes shot wide open.

"Jon David, it's okay, it's okay," said Joan Luke, his startled mother.

Gregory Luke jumped up from the chair and rushed over. Upon seeing his son, the retired Army colonel and Viet Nam veteran knew this wasn't mere pain. It was complete anguish. He rocketed out of the room to get help.

Jon David lay twisted, panting and writhing, screaming in synchrony with the waves of pain. His grip on his mother's hand was so tight that it would leave her with black-and-blue marks. "Nurse! Nurse!" she screamed with tears pouring from her eyes.

Gregory Luke manhandled a nurse into the room. She quickly administered a shot of morphine into his son's IV. Within a minute, the lieutenant slipped back into unconsciousness.

"Oh Greg! Oh Greg!" was all his wife could say as tears streamed down her face. He brought her into his arms and held her tightly for a long time. Tears poured from the tough, former war dog as well.

"Joanie," he said a while later, "we need to be strong; he'll need our strength to get through this."

She embraced him tighter in reply. "My God, my dear God..."

The nightmare that Greg and Joan Luke were now living had begun five days ago with a midnight call from Pete Bergstrom, Jon David's battalion commander. Bergstrom would always remember it as the toughest call he'd ever had to make. He had a soft spot in his heart for his brash young lieutenant, who never had a problem going toe-to-toe with him or any other flag officer if it meant improving the lives of his troops or the residents of Taji. Despite willing himself to remain in control, Bergstrom wept as he told Jon David's father the tragic news of the day in Taji that would change forever the life of the man they loved. A few hours later, the Lukes were flying to Germany to be with their son.

The following day, the Lukes returned to the hospital after spending the night at base lodging. They were relieved to see their son sleeping. Although it was against her husband's wishes, Joan insisted on helping the nurse give Jon David a sponge bath and change the bandages covering his wounds. The mothering instinct in her would not be denied.

The nurse came in pushing a cart loaded with a sundry of bandages and medical potions. She removed Jon David's bed sheet. "Oh, my God!" gasped Joan Luke. The extent of her son's wounds—the bloody stump where his left leg had been, the shredded right leg, coupled with his arm traumas, the cast on his broken wrist, missing teeth and broken jaw now wired shut—was too much for her to bear. She staggered out of his room, felt her world go black, and collapsed to the floor.

When she regained consciousness, Joan Luke appeared to have aged several years in a matter of minutes. After being helped to a chair in Jon David's room, she sat like a zombie for the rest of the morning without uttering a word. An occasional tear would fall from her cheek. Her beautiful boy was a mess.

Greg Luke spent the day at his son's side, grateful when Jon David's doctor took his wife to be with one of the hospital's counselors. At about three in the afternoon, he noticed his hand being gently squeezed by his son, who now had his eyes half open, looking at him. Colonel

Luke leaned over and kissed his soldier-son on the forehead. "I love you, son."

A tear rolled down Jon David's cheek. Since he couldn't talk with wired together jaws, he motioned for a tablet and pen. Under heavy sedation and racked with pain, in a shaky hand he wrote: NOT WORY. I BE OK. Greg Luke wept when he read his beloved son's words.

Two weeks later, Jon David awoke to his father's stern "colonel" voice. He and his brother only heard it when their father was angry.

"Doctor, it makes no sense. My son is in no shape to fly across an ocean."

"Sir, the maximum stay for wounded soldiers in Landstuhl is fifteen days."

"That's bull crap."

"Colonel Luke, Walter Reed is much better equipped to handle trauma cases like your son. Believe me, this is medically warranted. The C-17 medivacs are flying ERs, so he won't be in peril on the journey."

"Greg, let them do what they think is best," said Joan Luke, finally. Her remark ended the conversation.

Jon David was airlifted that night to Walter Reed Army Medical Center in Washington, DC. His parents had left Germany several hours before him on a commercial flight back to the states. They were there to greet him when he arrived at Walter Reed. Danny Luke, Jon David's kid brother, accompanied his parents. They tried to prepare him for the new reality that defined his brother.

# 4

THE INITIAL DAYS at Walter Reed were a blur, with Jon David being kept in a near comatose state through the miracle of modern-day sedatives and painkillers. After a week, the physicians eased off the medications, allowing him to come back to the world of awareness. Consciousness wasn't the best place to be. Pain lived there.

His hospital room, although basic, was decorated with flowers and cards from many well-wishers. He had a pile of letters on his night-stand from his troops and Pete Bergstrom, his battalion commander. His father read the letters to him, but only in the absence of his mother. Many of the words and subjects in them weren't meant for the delicate ears of mothers. Since his recollection of events on that terrible day in Taji had ended with the potter pulling him to safety, the letters filled in a lot of gaps regarding what had happened.

Jon David took particular satisfaction when learning the fate of Abdul Khalaf, the absent tribal leader who owned the tobacco shop in Taji. A village elder remembered seeing one of the insurgents' vans parked outside Khalaf's residence the night before. Subsequent inter-rogation involving more physical persuasion than actual questions by other tribal leaders and several irate residents who had lost family members yielded a confession. Khalaf acknowledged having what the local leaders described as "mixed loyalties." Helping the Arab "freedom fighters" proved to be a fatal mistake. His actions nearly killed Taji's respected lieutenant and many children. Abdul Khalaf was found in a field the next day; his bruised and battered body indicated his last hours on earth were in no way pleasant.

The wall that collapsed from the exploding RPG claimed six Iraqi children plus the life of his dear friend Haakim Al-Jamil. In addition to Haakim, Staff Sergeant Mario Frisby, Specialist Wade Gilpin, and Private Gary Fink were killed in action. Sergeant Bruce Steely was severely wounded and privates Larry Opperman and Jon Scudder each received some hot metal souvenirs. Ten civilians also succumbed. The battle came to an abrupt end shortly after Jon David and the potter exited the scene. The insurgents realized the element of surprise was over and quickly blended back in with the local populace. The entire skirmish was over in less than fifteen minutes. Classic AQI ambush and run.

The events of that day led to a litany of other sad stories. After the battle, a U.S. Army Civil Affairs unit was dispatched to Taji to offer restitution for the accidental deaths and damage. Many of the shops were chewed up by the three Browning machine guns as well as the insurgent's RPGs. The commander of the unit received spirited encouragement from Jon David's soldiers to make things right with the potter's family who left a wife of twenty-one years and three teenage children. He promised his full and immediate attention to the matter. Two days later, he paid in cash the maximum amount the Army allows for an accidental civilian death in Iraq—$2,500.

The Arab news network Al-Jazeera featured the potter's family on an evening news broadcast. The next day, they were found dead in their home, each bearing signature AQI traumas.

Jon David grimaced as his father read the letters. He was responsible for his soldiers, the children, and the townspeople and he had let them down. In retrospect, he realized he had made a typical lieutenant error of being on point instead of staying further back so he could've better led his squad during the attack. And, he should have known something was wrong when that damn tobacco merchant was missing.

In the days ahead, his mind would replay the battle repeatedly. Each replay ended with one glaring fact. He had lost his men. And for that, he would never forgive himself. The tears he shed for his men in the hospital in Germany began again. Now, they were accompanied by another form of pain—the kind of pain that comes in the dark of the night from a wounded soul.

From the day Jon David arrived at Walter Reed Army Medical Center, a multidisciplinary team was assigned to care for and oversee his recovery. The group included physicians skilled in every subspecialty he would need, nurses, occupational and physical therapists, nutritionists and a variety of essential supportive personnel including clergy, laboratory assistants and clerical staff. There was even a licensed clinical social worker to help him readjust to his new environment.

Despite the army of worker bees tending to him, Jon David didn't respond as well as other wounded soldiers returning from combat. The social worker explained to his parents how traumatic experiences produce a plethora of problems that affect each person in many different ways. Increasingly, he was troubled by fear and anxiety. Noises, like a dropped bedpan, would leave him shaking. Other times, he felt overwhelmed with gripping distress. Nights brought terrors. Vivid images of the battle, especially of Haady, the young boy staring lifelessly at him, robbed him of restful sleep. He shared these troubles with his doctor, who added post-traumatic stress disorder to his ills. With that came more pills called Selective Serotonin Reuptake Inhibitors, a fancy name for antidepressants. These pills brought side effects, including what Jon David sullenly called, "chemical neutering." *Hell,* he thought, *what does it matter, it's not like demand for your manhood is there anymore.*

Despite these medications, the pain, depression, panic attacks, and sleeplessness persisted, and, in some cases, intensified, resulting in a wicked short temper. Although his parents were once welcome guests, he now saw them as unbearable nuisances. Especially frustrating was communicating due to his jaw being wired shut. He hated writing messages on paper, and often got so annoyed that he'd rip the paper off the tablet, wad it up, and throw it across the room. Aborted interactions with his parents and assorted medical staff resulted in the floor being littered with mounds of trash.

The matter of his girlfriend didn't help. She came to visit during his fourth week at Walter Reed and gagged when she saw his stump. She tried to feign nonchalance, made her excuses, and left. Three days later, an orderly delivered a letter that had arrived in the mail. It was the first "Dear Jon" letter he had ever received. He never heard from her again. So much for true love, his cynical subconscious declared.

Being on a liquid diet took its toll. He dropped from a robust 203 pounds to 168 and his gaunt face made him look ten years older.

The start of his sixth week stateside brought some good news. His doctor walked in with his parents. "Good morning, Jon David. I just told your parents that we can remove the wires from your jaws. You'll be able to eat normal food and speak again."

"This is great news, son," his dad said excitedly. "Let's celebrate this day with pizza. While you're having the procedure done, we'll get one for lunch." The lieutenant nodded in agreement. The doc helped him to the wheelchair and wheeled him down the hall.

"We'll see you in about an hour," his mom said.

The good news of this milestone recovery event evaporated after the wires were removed. Jon David couldn't utter a word. Try as he might, nothing came out. His doctor examined his vocal chords. "Jon David, everything looks fine. Let's give it some time, and with therapy, I'm confident you'll be fine."

The cheerfulness of the physician couldn't overcome his disappointment, which turned to rage after he returned to his room. His parents came in holding a monster-sized pizza box. "Here you go, Jon David," said his mom, "let's dig in!" He grabbed the box and hurled it across the room. The box exploded on the wall, sending pizza slices everywhere. His parents stood there aghast. Jon David started beating the wall with his fists, breaking the wallboard with every blow.

"Jon David, for God's sake, what the hell are you doing?" boomed his father. He tried but failed to restrain his son. "Get me some help!" His wife ran in a panic from the room, screaming for assistance. It took four people to hold the lieutenant down. Only a sedative could calm him. The doc later explained what had happened regarding his vocal chords. Joan Luke spent the night crying inconsolably in her husband's arms.

Weeks passed. Despite gaining his voice back after working daily with a speech therapist, nothing seemed to matter anymore. The arch enemy in Jon David's recovery was chronic pain. It sat like a wolf, licking its chops, always hungry, devouring everything normal in his life. It caused fatigue, which lead to impatience, which lead to loss of motivation. It ate his sleep, keeping him up at night. It caused him to withdraw from all activities. It ate away at his immune system, leading to frequent infections. It chewed at his psyche, causing depression which, in turn, made his pain seem worse. And, it ate the last morsel of his Army career. Some amputees were allowed to stay in the Army, but with Jon David's merciless pain, leading men in combat was inconceivable. He could barely negotiate his way through a fast food menu. Besides, if other customers queued up behind him, they could be armed and dangerous. He couldn't drop his guard on them and order at the same time, so prudence demanded that he leave rather than face unnecessary risks.

He descended ever more into the depths of despair. Often, he would sit in his room, numbly watching the television. He had no interest in people and no plans for the future. All he had in abundance was an empty view of the world and his role in it. His anger and frustration were often leveled at his parents. He shocked his mother with frequent torrents of foul words. The toll on them was so evident that the team's social worker demanded they take a month off to recharge.

It was a long drive back to Roanoke for Gregory Luke. He listened to his wife's non-stop tirade on the three-hour trip without saying a word. Joan Luke's ranting could be distilled into one succinct sentence. She rued the day her sweet boy became a soldier.

After his skin wounds healed, Jon David underwent an intense physical therapy regimen at the Walter Reed Military Advanced Training Center for Soldier Amputees. The 31,000 square-foot rehabilitation center was considered to be the best in the world, offering state-of-the-art physical and occupational therapy, virtual reality systems, sports programs, and prosthetics training. This day, he had an appointment at the prosthesis laboratory. He waited as patiently as he could for his turn to be seen. A gray-haired African American technician with an easy smile walked in. "Are you Lieutenant Luke?"

"Yes, sir."

"C'mon back, and let's get you going. I got some fine toys to show you." Jon David smiled weakly in reply and started wheeling his wheelchair to the room. "The first step in getting you mobile is to fit your leg with a plastic socket using this here fancy CAD/CAM computer imager. You'll get what we call a transtibial prosthesis, which is for people with amputations below the knee. Having your knee is good. The ones missing the knee I fit with something called a transfemoral prosthesis. Them mothers come with microcomputers that you have to recharge each night like a cell phone. Costs Uncle Sugar a hundred grand. Your prosthesis will come with some sweet things called elastomeric gels that'll fit perfectly to your residual limb. It'll be almost as good as what you used to have."

"Thanks just the same, but I was partial to the original one."

"I know, young man, but I promise you'll be able to get around with what I'll give you. The days of those old "peg legs" are long over. C'mon, let's get it done."

A few weeks after being outfitted with his new leg, Jon David could move around with the assistance of crutches. He could pass for normal if he wore long pants and sleeved shirts. But mobility brought new and unexpected consequences. Among people, he experienced culture shock, where everyone had to be assessed as a potential threat. His senses were on hyper-alert, scanning faces, looking at objects discarded on the street as potential IEDs. A simple trip to a store would leave him mentally exhausted. Even the weather seemed far too cold after the sweltering days in Iraq.

The rebuilding of Lieutenant Luke would never be total. With his chronic pain and injured psyche, he was a shell of his once robust self. A modified version of a nursery rhyme took residence in his head, which he mentally repeated over and over:

> *Jon David sat on a wall.*
> *Jon David had a great fall.*
> *All the king's horses and all the king's men*
> *Couldn't put Jon David together again.*

On the day of his discharge, he met with his doctor. "Well, Jon David, we're cutting you loose today. You'll now go through our Warriors in Transition program. You still have a long road ahead of you. Just remember it's important to keep your spirits up."

"Thanks for all you've done, Doc," he said half-heartedly. "But, if this is the best that can be done, it's not encouraging."

"It'll get better. You'll have to keep up with your therapy though."

Jon David didn't feel like arguing. He knew the reality for the rest of his life would include some sort of pain, be it mental or physical. There were limitations to modern-day medicine. Not even the best surgeon in the world could excise the image of Haady on the street that day. Removing just that one image would give him many more nights of peaceful sleep.

To celebrate his discharge from Walter Reed, his parents threw a gala for him at their home in Roanoke. They went all out, inviting his high school friends and members from his West Point class. More than fifty people came to see him. After being there for less than fifteen minutes, Jon David gave his brother a world-class butt chewing for putting too much lighter fluid on the charcoal. He stormed out, leaving Danny in tears, and drove like a madman back to DC, cursing the whole way. He never considered the abandoned guests and family he left in his wake.

Six months after his last day in Iraq, First Lieutenant Jon David Luke was medically retired from the United States Army. He wept on the day of his "retirement." All that effort at the Academy, all the pride from wearing the uniform, and all the camaraderie with his soldier-brothers—gone. After a brief stint at Mologne House as an outpatient, he now lived on a modest monthly disability stipend in a sparse apartment near Walter Reed.

# 5

*Two years later…*

*Walter Reed Army Medical Center*
*Washington, DC*

JON DAVID SAT in the exam room fuming at the latest round of hell being visited upon him. This episode in his soap opera existence had begun innocently enough a week back when a two-inch long linear red mark, with its attendant pain, appeared on his right thigh about six inches above his knee. He knew the drill regarding this affliction. Shrapnel was working its way to the surface. He'd had several pieces of the metal removed in the last couple of years. Each of these events launched a round of arguments with his doctors. Jon David wanted them to extract all of the shrapnel from his body, particularly the numerous small bumps near the surface of his skin. The doctors sang in unison against this notion, arguing that removing embedded shrapnel can actually do more harm than good. The body seems to tolerate shrapnel pretty well, they added. He scoffed at the tolerance remark. Spend one day in my body and the acute pain would have you scrambling for your scalpels, he would counter. And so it went…

Jon David had another powerful reason to remove the shrapnel, but he would never bring it to the attention of the medical staff. Each of these flare-ups brought back all the memories of the wicked hot, razor-edged shards of metal tearing into his body. This touched off more nightmares. Lately, they were becoming alarmingly intense, leaving him utterly drained and in a bed of sweat-soaked sheets. In the first months after coming home, two shots of vodka at night would dull the bad dreams. After six months, he needed three shots, and then four. Now, it wasn't unusual for him to kill a fifth in the evening. His doctors warned of drinking being incompatible with the medications he was taking, but Jon David no longer cared. Anyone seeing him—broken, unshaved and downtrodden—would scarcely recognize the once cocky, high-spirited warrior that he had been less than three years ago.

A female doctor interrupted his thoughts, barging into the exam room while reading the latest lab report. The frown on her face was a cue for unfortunate news. Three days ago, the small red mark on his leg had blossomed into a fast-growing red-hot abscess. "What now?" Jon David said, providing the prompt for the woman to begin.

"Not good, Lieutenant," the spectacled doctor said. "Your high fever and raised white blood cell count indicate you have a staph infection. If we aren't careful, this could lead to a blood stream infection called septicemia. If that happens, it could be life threatening."

"Shit." There was nothing else to say.

"We're going to have to admit you and put you on aggressive intravenous antibiotics."

"Just give me a pill and let me out of here."

"Jon David, hear me, you could die from this," the alarmed doctor said, putting her hand on his to emphasize the point.

"So what?" he replied, wearily.

"I'm going to call for a room, and I think you should use this opportunity to talk to a counselor," she said in a comforting tone. "You've been through a lot, I know, but it'll get better." He gazed at her and wanted to laugh. *Lady, you haven't a clue,* he thought to himself. His 103-degree temperature zapped all his desire to get testy.

Jon David checked into the hospital that afternoon. How many times had he done this, he wondered. He'd lost count long ago. Heck, he thought, the count was over twenty-five or thirty by now. There were enough medications in his apartment to open a pharmacy. For extra spending money, he flirted with the thought of selling some of his pain medication on the local market, where choice pills would command some tall green. These days, however, he lived from pain pill to pain pill. The thought of parting with any of them was inconceivable.

While chewing on a few ice chips, he wondered when the next pain pill would be delivered. The intravenous drip of antibiotics felt like acid in his veins. He thought about pushing the nurse call button and demanding immediate relief, but with a sigh, he decided to wait ten minutes before lighting a fire under their butts. He reached under his blanket to check if the abscess had abated. When his fingers touched the oozy thing, it sent a lightning bolt back to his head. He silently mouthed the word OUCH! followed by the out-loud word "DAMN!" He looked again at the wall clock. Eight minutes to go. He put the call button in his hand. When the eighth minute passed, he'd hit that damn button like it was a rocket launcher. He closed his eyes to avoid seeing the second hand on the clock moving through every single second. God, how I want a drink, he thought. That wasn't exactly the truth. What he really wanted was an ocean of booze.

Four days in the hospital passed. A surgeon, two days before, had picked and probed at the abscess and let out a whoop of joy when he was rewarded with a half-inch piece of metal. It joined its brothers and sisters in a small glass jar Jon David kept.

His spectacled doctor came in with a big smile. "Jon David, I'm so happy!" she said, beaming like a schoolgirl. "We've beat it!" She handed the lab report to him as if he would know what it meant. "We can release you tomorrow, but you'll still have to take oral antibiotics for a while." He mustered a half-hearted smile, not wanting to kill her joy. "Did you see a counselor yet?" she asked while signing a form.

"I made an appointment for next week," he said, knowing he had no intention of going.

"That's great!" she replied as she exited his room, still bubbly over her medical prowess.

In reality, he hoped he'd contract the septi-whatever blood infection so it would make short work of him. His thoughts turned to his apartment. He wanted the taste of vodka or whiskey in his mouth. Tomorrow, he was going to party hearty. It would be a party only for two—his booze and him. The next day, he took a taxi to his apartment, with a brief stop at a liquor store. By eight that night, a fifth of vodka was consumed. By nine-thirty, a fifth of whiskey was half drained.

Jon David sat in his secondhand recliner, contemplating life while staring at some mindless nonsense on TV. He surveyed his dismal apartment, littered with piles of old pizza and Chinese food boxes and trash cans overflowing with emptied liquor bottles. *My mother would go into shock if she saw the damn place. But this is my life, and it'll only go downhill from here,* he thought, almost chuckling. He struggled to get on his feet and staggered into his apartment's tiny bedroom. His stump fiercely protested the jarring motions. He plopped on the bed, opened the drawer of his nightstand, and pulled out a civilian version of an M9 Beretta. He held the weapon in his hand and looked at it for a long while. He flipped off the safety and raised the pistol to his head. He held it there, finger on the trigger, until his hand started shaking. A voice within him spoke. *No, not this way, not this way.* His mind succumbed to the alcohol. He passed out on the bed, gun still in hand, and didn't wake for ten hours.

# 6

THE PHONE RINGING jarred Jon David awake. He picked it up and tersely said hello.

"Jon David, its Mom! Are you still sleeping?"

He lied. "No, Mom, I was just dozing off on the couch."

"Your brother is coming this weekend from Penn State and it would really be great if you came home too." He knew the difference between his mother's requests and her demands. This was the latter. There was a long pause…"Jon David, are you still there? Hello?"

"Yes, Mom, I'm here. When do you want me there?"

"Just come anytime on Sunday."

"All right, Mom."

"Well, I've got a hundred things to do, so I'll see you then. Sweetheart, are you okay?"

Another pause…

"Yes Mom, I'm fine."

"Okay then, see you here on Sunday."

Jon David hung up the phone with an exasperated sigh. The thought of another family gathering was the last thing on earth he wanted. It would take a massive effort to get "up" for the event and he simply didn't know if he could rise to the occasion. He lay in his bed, looking at cobwebs on the ceiling. His body was screaming in pain and his head throbbed with a full-blown hangover. He was too exhausted to move, too emotionally numb to care. As he lay there, the flashbacks of his parents seeing him in Germany came to his consciousness. It saddened him deeply the anguish he'd put his parents through, starting on the day his commander called suggesting they immediately fly to

Germany to be with their critically injured son. He remembered their hushed conversations and tears at his bedside when he awoke on the second day and his mother's loud gasp when a nurse removed his bed sheet to clean his wounds.

A jet flying overhead brought him back to the present. He looked at the Beretta lying on the bed. He thought about the world with its ceaseless killing and hatred and the evening newscasts blaring nothing but bad news. He always winced when the news anchor reported another bombing in Iraq. He thought of other lieutenants just like him and the devastating blow that comes to a leader when they lose one of their men. The violence and bad news wasn't limited to just that area of the world. It was global, endemic. People killing others for no reason in Africa, the economy in this country sliding downward, another horrific school killing…and just look at him—broken, battered, living on disability checks that would never elevate him to anything other than a dingy apartment existence. He let out a long sigh at the dismal tally, but the facts were the facts. The world sucked. His life sucked. Sucked big. *So much for life after the Purple Heart,* he cynically thought. *Your life will never be anything more than a sad country song.*

He made a decision. It was time to leave, time to check out of this sorry planet. No more half-ass attempts. He lay on the bed thinking about this. It felt completely right, except for one thing. Checking out would bring shame to his family. He simply could not do that. He thought some more, focusing again on the ceiling cobwebs.

His eyes suddenly went wide open—an epiphany came to him. *Stage it! Make it look like an accident.* His mind raced. *But how?* He would have to give this some more thought. But the decision to leave had been made and with this decision came a wave of exhilaration. He was back in control of his life. He'd found the ultimate way to reign victorious over his arch enemy, the pain. He must, he thought, get himself "up" for the family get-together this weekend. He wanted his parents to see him looking normal before he left his sorry existence behind.

# 7

JON DAVID PUT ON a skillful performance at his family's home, dishing out charm and acting every bit like the JD of old. He had even dispensed some of his old cockiness, his father would later proudly say.

He apologized to his brother Danny for his previous poor behavior and hugged him hard when forgiveness was granted. He stayed for three hours, and, upon leaving, hugged each of his family, telling them how much he loved them. They stood in the driveway waving, smiling, and thinking to themselves how well he was doing.

Jon David drove a couple of miles down the road, turned into an alleyway, parked his car and crumpled over the steering wheel, utterly exhausted from the ordeal. He reached into the glove compartment and pulled out a bottle of vodka. He took several gulps. After an hour, he'd regained his composure enough for the drive back to DC, where he collapsed on his bed.

The next morning came and he had business to tend to—an appointment with his Walter Reed doctor to renew his pain medications. Nothing would keep him from showing up. He had to have his best friends, the pills.

In the patient seating area, each passing moment elevated his annoyance. He hated waiting. He hated hospitals. He hated his broken body causing him to be here. He hated many things. A gray-haired veteran walked in, scanned the room, hustled over, and sat next to him. Jon David's anger rocketed. *Why in the hell did this old coot sit next to me? There are plenty of other vacant seats to be had.* His ire came close to exploding when the vet, who appeared to be in his late-fifties or early-sixties, tried to strike up a conversation.

"How you doing?" the man said in a friendly tone.

He returned the man's greeting with a half-hearted smile.

"My name's Jamie Spell. My wife, Penny, and I are visiting DC from Anchorage, Alaska. I ran out of pills, so here I am trying to get my prescription renewed. Are you from around here?"

Jon David fought the urge to get up and move to another chair. Conversing was the last thing he wanted. "No offense, sir, but I don't feel much like talking to you or anyone else."

The older vet's expression flashed to empathy. "That's no problem. I'll just sit here and leave you to your peace." He shifted his weight in his seat, exposing a prosthetic leg. Jon David couldn't help but notice.

"Did you lose it in battle?"

"I did. Khe Sanh, Vietnam. *Semper Fi.*"

Jon David pulled up his pants leg. "Iraq. Army Ranger. My name is Jon David Luke." He held out his hand and the older vet shook it. They sat in reflective quiet.

"I was stationed at Fort Richardson on my first tour. How are things back in Alaska?"

"Great! They got a new military mall and a big-ass regional hospital. Pretty sweet."

Jon David smiled in reply. Even this meager conversation drained him. The older man sat for a while before breaking the silence.

"Jon David, this may sound presumptuous, but I'd be honored if you'd come visit Penny and me in Anchorage. We have a big ol' house with plenty of space since the kids left. You can stay with us for as long as you like. I got a real nice cabin in the bush that you're welcome to use as well. It's accessible only by air—I can fly you out in my Super Cub and you can stay there all you want. You can do some serious thinkin' there, if you know what I mean."

Jon David looked at the man. He'd met him minutes ago and now the guy was inviting him to stay with him in Alaska? Despite his suspicions, he inexplicably found the offer to be tempting. He stared into the older man's eyes to see if he was being conned, but the old man looked him right back in the eye with an expression of utter genuineness.

"Are you serious?" Jon David finally asked.

"I truly am. We'll return to Anchor-town next week, on 12 December." He reached into his coat pocket, pulled out a pen, scribbled his name and cell phone number on a scrap piece of paper, and handed it to Jon David.

An orderly came out and scanned the room. "Mr. Luke…?"

Jon David waved, and before he stood up, extended his hand to the older man. "I just might take you up on your kind offer, sir." he said as they shook hands.

"Penny and I will count on it!" His blue eyes twinkled with joy. "Call me if you decide to visit. As you know, winter in Alaska has its own unique beauty."

Jon David nodded, got up, and began following the orderly. Near the exam room door, he turned and looked one last time at his new "friend." The older vet smiled and waved goodbye. He responded in kind. His mind transmitted a message: *we're going to Alaska.*

After getting renewed medicine scripts and prescriptions filled, Jon David drove back to his apartment. The more he thought about it, the more Alaska was the perfect "check out" point. There were a thousand ways to die there, all of which could look perfectly natural.

He smiled. He now had a plan, a good plan. Countless times he'd wished he would've died with honor on the battlefield rather than being the pathetic shell of a man he was today. He was a warrior and in Alaska he'd have the chance to die a warrior's death. His foe this time was pain. He'd kill it by killing himself. Then he'd be free of this miserable existence and its unrelenting assault on his manhood and psyche. He was now in control again, calling the shots, and being back in control felt mighty good. Soon he'd leave this crummy world and his family would still have their war hero. A true win-win situation if ever there was one.

He called the Spells the next morning, told them he was coming, and bought a one-way plane ticket the same day.

# 8

THE PIPER "SUPER Cub," built in 1962, rose into the frigid Alaska morning air, bound for a cabin near the Talachulitna River about seventy-five miles northwest of Anchorage. Its high-lift wing and powerful 150-horsepower Lycoming engine made short work of the runway, heading skyward in less than 600 feet. Six minutes in the air and now at 2100 feet, Jon David and Jamie Spell had the best seats in Anchorage for seeing Mount Susitna and the magnificent Alaska Range. Factoring in the plane's 120 miles-per-hour cruising speed and a slight headwind, touchdown at the cabin's airstrip would be in about forty-five minutes.

Jon David sat behind Jamie in the tandem-seated aircraft. Since the plane didn't have an intercom system, the deafening roar of the engine reduced conversation to nothing more than hand motions. That was fine with Jon David. He found the constant drone to be mesmerizing, somehow taking his mind off his pain. Jamie made a few gestures at Mount Susitna, the "Sleeping Lady" and Jon David gave him a thumbs up to indicate he saw it too. In the cold, crystal-clear winter air, the mountain was stunningly vivid and beautiful. Like his pilot, Jon David loved this land.

This was the second trip he was making to the cabin with Jamie since arriving in Alaska a short week ago and he was eager to return. The first time had been brief, to get him acquainted with the cabin and the area. Even a simple, non-electrified, no-running-water cabin has nuances to learn, such as how to start and keep a fire going in the cast iron stove. At 30 below, fire meant life. Equally essential, Jamie said with a wry smile, was to know the location of the pee bottle, an item of critical importance to a man his age. He was too old, he mused, to make a run to the outhouse twice a night in below-zero weather. Doing it would "get his nuts to chattering." Jon David found he liked this man and his wife Penny quite deeply. They were some of the nicest people he'd ever met. They gave him space and never once asked about his life or his troubles, even when he requested a trip to the local liquor store.

He was amused at how the Spells had "adopted" his parents as well. Penny and Jon David's mother were already trading recipes and talking about getting together in the summer. Jamie and his dad struck up a quick relationship too. A couple of nights ago, he overheard Jamie speaking to his father on the phone. "All the boy needs is some solitude to sort things out," Jamie had said. From the tone of the conversation following, it appeared his dad agreed.

What all these good-intentioned people didn't know was that Jon David had already found his earthly "check out" point. It would be at the cabin on the night before Christmas.

Jamie set the Cub down without a bump on the eight-hundred-foot frozen airstrip like he had done it a thousand times. Maybe he had, Jon David thought. He was an outstanding pilot. They exited the plane and were greeted by a ten-mile-per-hour breeze that brought the wind chill temperature down to 49 below. *Christ almighty,* Jon David thought as he grabbed his gear and a small plastic sled from behind his seat. This was quite a change from the sweltering days in the Iraqi sand box. Jamie had him superbly outfitted for the surroundings—he'd struck gold, as he called it, twenty-one years ago when Alyeska Pipeline Service Company, the operator of the oil-carrying eight-hundred-mile-long Trans Alaska Pipeline, had a massive "garage sale." Jamie bought enough arctic gear at fire sale prices to equip an army. After twenty years, he still talked about that day, acting as if he'd won some sort of arctic lottery. Jon David appreciated the warmth of the finest down parkas and bibs ever made.

He had provisions for three days, but knowing Penny, she had probably packed enough food in the Igloo chest to last ten. He smiled at the thought. He was grateful they weren't disappointed when he asked to stay at the cabin on Christmas Eve. In fact, Jamie seemed to light up when Jon David suggested the idea.

Jamie gave him a big hug. "I'll pick you up at the same time on Christmas day." He climbed into the plane. With the winter sun up for only six hours, he didn't have much time to get back to town before darkness set in. A few seconds later, the still-warm engine sputtered to life and was purring again. Jamie fed it more fuel and the plane's noisy propeller instantly responded, biting the air and moving the little plane forward. Jon David stepped back and shielded himself from the prop's wind blast and then watched as the aircraft taxied and leapt back into the air. After a few more moments, the frigid temperature cancelled the notion of lingering.

It amazed him how quiet it suddenly became. The ever-present DC bustle made him forget how quiet "quiet" really was. Here, he was sixty-five miles away from the nearest road and likely the same distance from the closest human. *That suits me just fine,* he thought. He grabbed the rope of the plastic sled holding his supplies and headed to the cabin which was about five-hundred feet away. The snow crunched loudly in protest to each step that he made. Every noise in the Alaska bush seemed to be heightened. Quiet, Jon David realized, was kind of scary.

After ten strenuous minutes, he reached the cabin. Jamie and Penny spent three summers building it nearly three decades ago. Since there were no roads, and with the airstrip being too short for a heavy airlifter, they had to haul the building materials to the site in the dead of winter by snow machine. Construction of the cabin was a family event. Their two boys and daughter proved to be enthusiastic apprentice carpenters. Jamie said it was a wonderful way for his family to bond. All of them had a powerful affinity for the little place simply known as "the cabin." Penny had wanted to name it something grand, but no eloquent name ever stuck.

Though humble by city standards, with no running water or electricity, in the bush it, was the equivalent of a castle. The cabin was built on pilings and its walls were made of spruce logs. It measured twenty feet wide by twenty-six feet long, with a sleeping loft that covered half of those dimensions. To shed the snow, it had a sharp forty-five-degree angled green-colored metal roof, which extended out to cover a six-foot porch. Four equilateral triangular-shaped windows were on the front wall near the apex. They flooded the interior with sunlight during the day.

The cabin was heated by a three-hundred pound cast iron stove. There was an enormous pile of firewood next to the deck to fuel it. Jamie laughed about how hauling the "blasted contraption" sixty-five miles in from the road nearly killed him, but the simple unit looked like it would last for a hundred years. Even though their children were now grown with kids of their own, collecting and chopping timber for firewood was still a Spell family tradition. A triple burner propane stove completed the "major" appliances. The "restroom" was thirty feet away from the cabin and had a crescent-moon cutout in the door. Jon David laughed when he learned an important Alaska Bush fact: In the middle of winter, the best toilet seat in the world is Styrofoam because of its excellent insulation properties. Sitting on bare wood at thirty below will quickly freeze your unmentionables.

Jamie told him how a Marine buddy had lost this parcel of land to him in a poker game back in Viet Nam. His bud's family homesteaded one hundred and sixty acres in the late 1940s and willed it to their only son. Jamie's eyes twinkled at telling how his friend ran out of money and bartered the land for poker chips. They decided an acre in that godforsaken place was worth ten bucks. Jamie won the pot and thirty acres. His friend dutifully had a choice piece of land carved from the homestead, and properly recorded it in Jamie's name. Three weeks after the deed arrived, his poker buddy had died instantly when a Viet Cong mortar shell found his foxhole at Khe Sanh.

On a whim, following his discharge from the Marine Corps after losing his leg, Jamie decided to go see his "property" in Alaska. He was stunned at the Eden his friend had ceded to him. It didn't take Jamie long to decide he belonged in Alaska. He settled in the "big city" of Anchorage with its fifty-thousand residents and found work teaching math at a high school. A year later, one of his colleagues persuaded him to go on a blind date with a "cute" third grade teacher named Penny. They were married within six months. Thirty years, and three children and ten grandchildren later, they still acted like newlyweds.

Jamie told Jon David he couldn't wait to show him the place in the summer. The "Tal"—short for Talachulitna River—was only a hundred feet away from the cabin. Its crystal clear water teemed with eight types of fish—five species of salmon: kings, silvers, reds, pinks, and chum, along with trout, grayling, and char. He swore his little piece of heaven was a fly fisher's "dream come true," and the season lasted from May all the way to mid-September. He beamed when saying the Tal was protected from human encroachment by the Skwentna River. The Tal drained into the Skwentna, which was a shallow, braided stream, unsafe for many to traverse except for an occasional expert river captain in a jet-powered shallow-draft boat. It was far easier for the hordes to go to other state rivers that had better accessibility. The beauty of the river and wildlife preservation was thus assured.

Jon David didn't have the heart to tell Jamie that he wouldn't be there for any summer fishing. In another era of his life, he would've eagerly counted down the days for a wilderness visit with the Spells. However, he had his own agenda to tend to, which came with a clock that was ticking down to his special "D-day"—departure day.

His plan to exit was, he thought, quite clever and certainly would look to all like a terrible accident. He conjured up the idea as Jamie went through the cabin drill on his first visit. The cast iron stove would be his salvation.

For five months a year, the warmth from the squat, log-burning stove made staying at the cabin possible. Located mid-way along the cabin's right wall, the black-colored piece of iron had a feed door large enough to accommodate an impressive-sized log. From a cold start, it took about three hours to get the cabin warm in subzero weather. Incredibly, if you didn't keep an eye on the burn rate of the logs, the inside could rocket to ninety-five degrees. Jamie used a combination of birch and spruce logs to fuel the fire. Both were easy to light and provided a nice hot fire. They also left a good bed of coals to get through the night. Birch logs were Jamie's favorite. When burned, they produced one of the most delightful aromas in nature. Jamie said it was his favorite brand of incense.

The secret to having a good fire, Jamie instructed Jon David, was to control the fire's burn rate. Give it too much oxygen and the logs will burn like a bonfire; too little oxygen cause them to halfheartedly smolder. He pointed to a paper on the wall next to the wood stove. It was a list of steps needed to light and then control the fire. As Jon David stared at those instructions on his first visit to the cabin, a light bulb came on in his head. Here was the perfect solution, his ticket for checking out…

Jon David hoisted the Igloo from the sled and tossed it up the four steps on the cabin's porch. Next came his backpack and a plastic jug holding a gallon of water, which was already starting to freeze. He grabbed the rail and awkwardly started to climb. Negotiating stairs covered with snow and ice was tricky with his fake leg. He turned the always unlocked door knob and opened the door. The cabin was as cold inside as it was outside. After bringing in the gear, the first priority would be to get the fire going. His aching body would welcome the warmth.

After three hours of hovering over the iron stove, Jon David felt comfortable enough to remove his parka and bib. He reached into his backpack and pulled out a pair of jeans and a thick wool sweater and quickly put them on. He then went to the Igloo chest and grabbed a container with the hand-written word STEW on it. He pulled open a drawer in the "kitchen," got out an iron skillet, and dumped in the generous portion of stew Penny had made for him. He then placed the skillet on the stove's flat cooking surface. Within minutes, its heat did its job and Jon David began devouring the stew straight from the pan, bachelor style. It was one of the most delicious meals he'd ever eaten.

A now sated appetite and the pleasant stew-and-wood scented air made him drowsy. He yawned and decided to turn in early, heading up the stairs to the queen-sized bed in the loft. He unloaded his backpack and methodically placed ten plastic pill bottles on the nightstand. Following this came the bottles of vodka and whiskey and then his ever-present Beretta. To his surprise, he found a small gift-wrapped package. He smiled and left it in the pack, deciding not to open it until Christmas Eve. He opened each medicine bottle, took out a pill, and tossed them into his mouth. He washed them down with a long swig of vodka. He lay there thinking about his plan for tomorrow, going over every detail with the military precision he had been taught at West Point.

The D-day plan was genius. It had hit him when Jamie showed him how to use the stove's chimney damper. The damper, slightly under-sized and made of a perforated cast-iron disk, was mounted inside the metal shaft exiting the stove. It formed a butterfly valve inside the pipe and was used to help regulate the stove's burn rate and to seal the stove shut when it wasn't in use. A second damper higher up on the vertical section of the stove pipe was there to shut down the stove in case of a chimney fire and to keep the critters out in the summer.

It dawned on Jon David that after the fire goes out during its smoky stage, the coals go on burning nearly smokeless for hours, giving off heat and...*gases*. He remembered from Army training the adamant rule of no charcoal grilling being allowed indoors, to include the use of Hibachi cooking grills. The burning charcoal from these units produces the deadly gas carbon monoxide and the generation of this gas often continues long after you assume the coals are extinguished. The odor-less, colorless carbon monoxide gas has an attraction to hemoglobin in the blood that's over two-hundred-fifty times greater than oxygen. Only eight hundred parts-per-million can kill a person in just two or three hours.

To stage an accident, all he had to do was get the fire in the stove going until it had a nice bed of coals, and then close the damper and crack open the log-feed door. After waiting outside for a couple of hours for the gases to reach lethal levels, he would go back into the cabin, reopen the damper, close the feed door, and then go to bed. In a short while, the gases would do their work, and his sad existence would be painlessly over. The subsequent autopsy would reveal acute carbon monoxide poisoning. With the stove's damper and feed door in their proper positions, it would look like an accident, similar to the numer-ous cases of carbon monoxide poisoning he knew occurred each year in Alaska.

He sighed at the thought of Jamie finding him lifeless and likely frozen the next day, but Jamie was a combat veteran, so it wouldn't be the first time he'd seen someone in that way. It was a lousy thing to do to his newfound friend, but he had no choice. The decision to leave had been made. The "big suck" that defined his existence simply had to stop.

Jon David absently reached over to his nightstand to fetch the vodka. He drained the bottle, closed his eyes, and hoped for a night free of dreams.

# 9

*The day before Christmas...*

JON DAVID WOKE early, or so he thought, since it was still dark outside. A quick look at his watch proved him wrong. It was already nine in the morning. The winter sun is lazy in the Northland and would take another hour to announce its presence. His body checked in with all its aches and pains and his belly joined the chorus, loudly broadcasting that it was time for breakfast. An hour later, after another round of pills, some whiskey, the fire once more blazing, and a stomach now content with a full load of pancakes and genuine Alaska birch syrup, Jon David was feeling relatively good as he contemplated how this was the last day of his life.

He decided to pass the morning at the wood plank table, working on a jigsaw puzzle. On his first visit to the cabin, Jamie had plucked the puzzle off a shelf, dumped the contents on the table, and got the edges completed along with a few more pieces before it was time for them to go. He said putting puzzles together was a favorite pastime when his grandkids came to visit. They'd stay up working intently on them until well after midnight in the summer. Jon David soon found himself acting like one of the grandkids, getting absorbed in putting the puzzle together. It was a mountain scene, probably a picture of the Alaska Range. He focused on the dark pieces. Hours passed.

He closed his eyes to give them a break and then took a moment to admire the table's six chairs, which all looked a bit different from each other. Penny had made each of them from willow branches she and the kids collected along the banks of the Tal. They are quite comfortable, he thought as he resumed working on the puzzle. After another ten pieces were solved, Jon David took in a long breath, exhaled, and gazed out the window at the stunning forested landscape.

After a while, his attention shifted to his thoughts…he wondered if he should make amends with God, but quickly dismissed the notion as folly. There was no God, he reminded himself. No God would allow the bloody hell he experienced in Taji. All there was on this planet was suffering. He smiled when remembering a bumper sticker on an old car—*Life's a bitch, and then you die.* How true. No, he had nothing to say to someone who didn't exist. He snorted and looked upward, speaking in a contempt-laden voice. "Hey God, even if I'm wrong about your sorry ass existence, I'll just invoke the words of the poet Heine. *'God will forgive me. That's his job.'* So, what say you about that?" He listened for a moment. Nothing infiltrated the silence. "Yeah, that's just what I figured."

His dark ramblings persisted.

More than ever, he thought, "evil" was like a bully, pummeling "good" without mercy. Just the suffering of one person begged the question of why. What did his beloved soldiers ever do to warrant their fate? He lived his life with honor and integrity and what did he get for it? Shit. Anger welled up and he felt the urge to have a drink. But, the booze was upstairs and not worth the effort to retrieve. "To hell with it all," he said aloud, and went back to assembling the puzzle.

Before he knew it, evening approached. He made another visit to the Igloo and pulled out a container with beef stroganoff written on it. Underneath the hand-drawn label was a smiley face. Jon David couldn't help but smile as he shook his head. Mothers are the same everywhere, he mused. Twenty minutes later, he was dining on another splendid meal. Penny was a gourmet. She made something as pedestrian as stroganoff taste grand. He remembered the small gift-wrapped package they'd put in his backpack and decided to open it. That would give him a good reason to visit his bottle of whiskey. As he lumbered up the stairs, his leg ached from the prosthetic. He went for the bottle first, and then sat down on the bed to open the gift.

The smile on his face evaporated when he saw its contents—a gold cross and chain. He brought the cross close to his eyes, stared at it for a while, and threw it with disgust to the floor. He knew the Spells meant well, but giving him a cross was insulting. *How dare they ram their beliefs down my throat! Do they think the poor heathen can be won over to their views with a cross?* His shaking hand reached for the whiskey and he took several gulps. Soon, the magic elixir did its work. He fell asleep on the bed. Four hours later, the little Iraqi boy's lifeless staring eyes invaded his sleep. Jon David woke up gasping.

He looked at his watch and recoiled in shock upon seeing the time. "Shit! Shit, shit, shit!" He had nearly blown it by passing out. He got up, started to reach for his pain pills, and stopped. *No,* he thought, *no pills tonight. The lab results will not suggest that you could've died from an overdose.* He grabbed the empty vodka bottle and put it in his pocket. He left the whiskey, not wanting to arouse suspicion if alcohol showed up on the lab panels and no liquor bottles were found. He stood up shakily, his stump now singing in agony, and walked over to the slightly open loft window. He closed it securely and went downstairs. His mission now entered the execution phase.

After struggling down the stairs, Jon David labored over to the cast iron stove. He opened the feed door and was delighted to see a nice display of coals glowing in the firebox. Perfect, he thought—at least one break had come his way tonight. He moved to the front of the cabin, took his parka and bibs off pegs on the wall, got dressed, and went back to the stove. He flipped the damper shut, and cracked open the log feed door to let the gases come into the room. He glanced at his watch to note the time, picked up a willow chair, and walked out to the cabin's porch. He closed the door behind him, reached into his pocket, pulled out the vodka bottle, and flung it as hard as he could into the woods. Snow began falling as he settled into the chair, waiting for the deadly gas to do his bidding.

Earlier in the day, Jon David had decided he would focus only on the good years of his life while waiting for the gas to rise to lethal levels. He'd start with his earliest memories and continue until his first day at West Point.

He thought about his parents and their love for him. His kid-brother and their sibling spats and triumphs…family vacations…growing up in Roanoke: baseball, football, nights spent chasing fireflies, looking at the stars, and sleeping out in the backyard tent. His first kiss. The first time he made love to a girl. His handsome, powerful, pain-free body. Good times. All long gone. Tears streamed down his face. "Thank you, Mom. Thank you, Dad. Goodbye, Danny." His exhaled breaths formed big, visible moisture clouds before mixing with the bitter-cold air. His teeth were now chattering in the subzero cold. With a shaking hand, he pulled back the sleeve of his parka, and looked at his glow-in-the-dark analog watch. He'd been outside for almost three hours! He struggled to his feet, beat his arms together to get his blood going, picked up the chair, and headed inside.

Jon David quickly undressed, hanging the winter gear back on the wall pegs. He kicked off his boots, and carried the chair back to its proper place. Next, he went to the stove, reopened the damper and closed the feed door. He stopped for a minute to look around. One last check for loose strings. Everything appeared okay. The room had a slight smoky smell, but nothing untoward. He struggled upstairs and checked the loft. The cross gift was on the floor, so he picked it up and placed it on the nightstand. After removing his pants and prosthetic leg, he crawled into bed. There was nothing more to say, to think about, to cry for, to hope for. He had failed his men, those little Iraqi boys, and ultimately, he had failed in the game of life. He was ready for the peace that would shortly be his. Sweet, dream-free, pain-free, worry-free peace…he closed his eyes on the last night of his life.

Deep into the night, Jon David woke with a start. Something was wrong.

Voices…he was hearing *voices* downstairs! A peculiar soft-colored light emanated from down there as well, bright enough for Jon David to see without a flashlight. He quickly put on his prosthetic leg and pants, grabbed his Beretta, and climbed down the stairs, flipping off the pistol's safety as he went. When he got to the bottom of the stairs, his gun was up and he was looking for targets. Military training had kicked in. He was once more a highly capable marksman. He turned to face the center of the room, finger on the trigger. His mouth dropped open in shock at what he saw…

# 10

HE BLINKED HARD, as if it could somehow reset his eyes. *"What the hell!"* he bellowed in disbelief at the sight of five human-like figures before him.

"Hello, Jon David," one of them said. "Please join us. We've been waiting for you."

The figures were sitting in Penny's willow chairs. The chairs had been moved from the table and were arranged in a semicircle in the center of the cabin. An unoccupied chair was sitting on the opposite side, facing them.

Looking closer, Jon David could see they were humans, but each was glowing from head-to-toe with auras that looked like bright neon lights! Even more amazing was they each glowed in a different color. The one on the left, a middle-aged male, was shimmering in a purple color with flashes of sky blue. To his left sat an ancient-looking man with a stunning silver-colored aura. Subtle gold hues were dancing about the edges of his aura. At the center of the semicircle was a younger man ablaze in a bright gold-colored luminescence. Next to him was an elderly woman angelically aglow, in white with occasional flits of green and orange. The last form on the right radiated a soft yellow. Jon David couldn't tell if the yellow one was male or female.

The gold one raised his right arm and motioned to the empty chair. "Please sit down, Jon David," he said, in a calm, pleasant-sounding baritone voice.

"Who are you people?" Jon David replied in military-style terseness, ignoring the gold one's invitation. His Beretta was still leveled at them.

"We're friends," the gold one replied, making a slight gesture with his right hand to the empty chair again.

Jon David hesitated for a few moments and looked again at each one, scanning them to see if they were carrying weapons. He looked as best he could at each of their faces, which were partially obscured by their auras. They didn't show any threatening signs. In fact, they all looked quite calm and friendly. The wrinkled man was smiling at Jon David as if they were old friends. The purple one also gestured for Jon David to sit down.

Another long pause…then Jon David lowered his weapon. "Okay, sure. Why the hell not?" he said in an exasperated tone. He walked over to the chair and plopped down. "So, what do you ETs want? If you're here to beam me up to the spaceship, you might want to find another person who gives a damn. Besides," he said as he pulled up his pants leg, "this human unit, as you can see, is damaged."

"We're not aliens, Jon David," replied the soft-voiced white-glowing lady with a hearty laugh that accentuated all the wrinkles on her maternal-looking face. "We simply want to talk with you."

Jon David wasn't buying her friendly manner. "I have nothing to say to you or anyone else. I'll thank you kindly to get up and get the hell out of here." He stole a quick glance at the iron stove. He could hear from the crackling sound that more logs had recently been added. The gold one caught his glance and spoke.

*"One who doesn't enter by the door…but climbs up some other way… is a thief and a robber."*

Jon David's mind reeled in shock. What? He knew! The gold one *knew* about the plan to check out! What the *hell…*? "Who are you?" he snarled, angry at this intrusion into his life.

*"I am the door,"* the gold one said. *"If anyone enters in by me, he will be saved, and will go in and…will find pasture. Wide is the gate and broad is the way that leads to destruction, and many are those who enter in by it. Narrow is the gate, and restricted is the way that leads to life! Few are those who find it."*

The purple one then spoke. "For many, a longing for death comes when they hear Spirit calling them home. In your case, all you have is a desire to escape and nothing more."

"What I do with my life is my own damn business. So, I ask again, why are you here?"

"Because you asked for us," the gold one said with a melancholy sigh flitting across his face. His aura got a bit smaller with the reply.

"What are you talking about? I didn't ask for anything, much less for a bunch of glowing...whatever the hell you are."

The yellow one perked up. "What is rule number three?"

Jon David's mouth dropped open. *How in the hell did they know the rules?* His mind raced back to his Army ritual, and he silently ran through the rules. *Rule one... Stay together. Rule two... Vigilance.* Then rule three... *Don't die.*

Jon David was speechless. His mind was spinning. The yellow figure spoke again in a voice sounding neither masculine nor feminine. "What comes after rule three?"

Jon David's brain was near overload. He searched his tangle of thoughts. After rule three, what? Finally, the answer came to him. *"Sweet Jesus, please bless us with your divine protection,"* he said softly, bowing his head as he spoke the words. Tears rolled down his face. He wiped the tears away, feeling ashamed for breaking down. "So, are you saying you're here to help me?"

The gold man nodded.

"Well," Jon David said angrily, "you're a little late. I lost four men— where the hell were all of you then? And it's been two years since that day. You guys must have a helluva liberal vacation policy."

The purple one spoke calmly in a deep, but friendly voice. "Do you remember Ecclesiastes in the Bible? *"For everything there is a season, and a time for every purpose under heaven."*

Jon David pondered the words. "So, are you saying my men died because it was their time? They were good people with families. And that little boy Haady and the other kids—why were they supposed to die? And why did you wait so long to come to me?"

*"It isn't for you to know times or seasons,"* said the gold one.

The purple man then spoke with empathy in his voice. "You weren't ready to speak to us until now."

"What do you want from me?"

The silver one replied in a high, old man's raspy voice. "To fulfill the purpose of your existence—God's divine plan for you."

"I no longer believe in God, not after what I've seen and been through."

"That's okay," said the purple one, "you soon will."

Jon David just looked at him and didn't reply. It was dawning on him that he wasn't dreaming. They seemed earthly—and weren't going to be shooed away. He turned his attention to the others. "So, what are your names?"

"Our names are not important," the yellow one said. "Our words are what matters."

Jon David decided he'd let it go at that. He'd simply name them by the color of light each was emitting. He looked at them, one by one, and issued a demand. "Prove to me there is a God."

The gold one sighed. *"Why does this generation seek a sign?"*

The old woman, Whitie, put her hand on Gold's arm and spoke softly. *"I was out walking in the early morning. All of a sudden I felt very uplifted, more uplifted than I had ever been. I remember I knew timelessness and spacelessness and lightness. I did not seem to be walking on the earth. There were no people or even animals around, but every flower, every bush, every tree seemed to wear a halo. There was a light emanation around everything and flecks of gold fell like slanted rain through the air. This experience is sometimes called the illumination period."*

She paused for a moment, as if summoning the right words to rise to the surface. In a soft and reasonable voice, she went on. *"The most important part of it was not the phenomena: the important part of it was the realization of the oneness of all creation. Not only all human beings—I knew before that all human beings are one. But now I knew also a oneness with the rest of creation. The creatures that walk the earth and the growing things of the earth. The air, the water, the earth itself. And, most wonderful of all, a oneness with that which permeates all and binds all together and gives life to all. A oneness with that which many would call God."*

Yellow then added, "Of God and wind I have not seen, yet I am touched by both."

Silver raised his hand, wanting to speak. Even through his silvery aura, Jon David could see that his face was old and wrinkled like a prune, but he had a glint in his eyes and enthusiasm in his voice.

"*Before the universe was born, there was something in the chaos of the heavens,*" Silver began. "*It stands alone and empty, solitary and unchanging. It is ever present and secure. It may be regarded as the Mother of the universe. Because I do not know its name, I call it the Tao. If forced to give it a name, I would call it 'Great.' Because it is Great means it is everywhere. Being everywhere means it is eternal. Being eternal means everything returns to it. Tao is great. Heaven is great. Earth is great. Humanity is great. Within the universe, these are the four great things. Humanity follows the earth. Earth follows Heaven. Heaven follows the Tao. The Tao follows only itself.*"

Silver looked at Gold, who nodded in agreement.

The old man went on. "*Since the beginning of time, the Tao has always existed. It is beyond existing and not existing. How do I know where creation comes from? I look inside myself and see it.*"

Yellow added to Silver's comment. "The poet Emerson said it well—'God enters by a private door into each individual.'"

"Well," said Jon David, "I've never had such an epiphany."

Silver threw back his head in a bellow of laughter. "Jon David, most would consider this to be a passable epiphany." The others laughed heartily at the old man's remark, nodding their heads in agreement. It was clear they enjoyed each other's company. In the middle of a room full of glowing people, the irony of Jon David's epiphany remark hit home. Despite himself, he couldn't subdue a sheepish grin. These people, he thought, were easy to like. He quietly leaned over and put the Beretta on the floor.

# 11

"ALL RIGHT," SAID Jon David, "for the sake of argument, let's say there is a God. So, where exactly do you find him?"

Whitie addressed this question. *"You can find God if you will only seek—by obeying divine laws, by loving people, by relinquishing self-will, attachments, negative thoughts and feelings. And when you find God it will be in stillness. You will find God within."*

Gold smiled at Whitie and then turned to Jon David. *"Ask, and it will be given you. Seek, and you will find. Knock, and it will be opened for you. I tell you, keep asking, and it will be given you. Keep seeking, and you will find. Keep knocking, and it will be opened to you. For everyone who asks receives. He who seeks finds. To him who knocks it will be opened."*

Yellow coughed demurely and spoke. "Buddha said that meditation brings wisdom, and lack of meditation brings ignorance. Know well what leads you forward and what holds you back, and choose the path that leads to wisdom. Jon David, you've but to listen to hear the still, small voice within. Instinctively, you knew you could no longer continue on the path you were on, but checking out, as you call it, is not the right path to choose. The right path—the right action—is to find a path that includes God."

"All right," said Jon David, "again, for the sake of argument, let's say there is a God. And if there is a God, why is there all the suffering in the world, the hatred, and people being killed?" A lump came to his throat as he went on. "My men, those… little boys?"

Purple touched Silver's arm, indicating he would answer the question. "There is an old story about five blind people who came upon an elephant. One felt its side and proclaimed, *'This is a wall.'* Another touched the trunk and said, *'No! This is a huge serpent.'* The next felt the flapping ear and said, '*You are all wrong, this is a huge fan.*' The person next to him felt the tusks and said, '*It is a spear.*' '*No, you are all wrong!*' said the most confident of the group, who was feeling a leg. '*It is obviously a tree.*' They spent the rest of the day in heated discussion, each clinging to their own myopic perspectives."

Purple let this story sink in for a few moments. "Jon David, you've lived your life in such a way. The 'absolute truths' you see are, in fact, the deceptive nature of half-truths. You touch the proverbial leg, or tail, or ear, and proclaim, 'this is not God, it couldn't be with all the suffering, all the pain...that dead little boy and his friends.'"

"So, you're telling me that all the suffering, the death of my men and the boys, it was all supposed to happen?"

They all nodded their heads with an affirmative yes.

"Why? How could their dying and my suffering serve any purpose?"

Whitie answered with a simple reply. "*People see themselves as the center of the universe and judge everything as it relates to them. Naturally you won't be happy that way. You can only be happy when you see things in proper perspective: all human beings are of equal importance in God's sight, and have a job to do in the divine plan.*"

Yellow piped up. "All the events in your life, all the good and the bad, all the triumphs and losses, your men, the boys, all of it, have served a divine purpose."

"For what—what *divine* purpose?" Jon David asked tersely, looking Yellow in the eye.

"All the events in your life, all the sacrifices of your friends, the good times and the bad, got you here, Jon David. It got you to where you are now."

"Sorry, I don't buy it. No God would cause such suffering. And, if everything truly did get me to where I am now, then I have to tell you, this 'now' is a pathetic place."

Purple pointed to the cabin's table. "Do you see the puzzle? It's made of a thousand pieces, but each of the pieces is unique and can only fit in the one spot meant for it. The pieces have different colors, some light, some dark. When they all come together, they form the puzzle's beautiful picture. And so it is with life. A beautiful life can only come from a palette of darks and lights."

Jon David thought about this. *Could there be divine reason for all the events in his life?* It didn't seem possible.

Purple broke the silence. "Think of your life as a puzzle. Right now, you have too few pieces of the puzzle assembled for you to see the whole picture. But, over a lifetime, when all the pieces of love, hate, anger, good, evil, bad, dark, light—when they all gradually come together, there will be a beautiful picture, and it will be the picture of your life. And, Jon David, there is one important thing to remember about the puzzle forming your life. Your puzzle, like the puzzle of every other human being, has one very special piece. That piece is called God. People try to put other pieces in where only the God piece goes—drugs, alcohol and the like. But, in the end, the puzzle will never be completed, for you or anyone else, until the God piece is put into its proper position."

Jon David nodded at the words. He thought about his endless and unyielding grief and then looked at Purple. "Your story sounds fine for someone who is whole, but too much has happened to me. I'm afraid the light within me is gone. You can't see a puzzle in the darkness, no matter how complete or beautiful it is."

"You are right," Purple said quietly, with empathy in his voice. "The light you once had will never shine again. But, with faith, you will discover a new light within you, and this light will shine just as brightly as the one before. You will see."

"All I feel is emptiness."

That remark sparked Silver to jump in. "Good! Empty is good," he said with an impish grin.

"How can emptiness possibly be good?"

*"Thirty spokes are joined together in a wheel,"* said the old man, *"but it is the center hole that allows the wheel to function. We mold clay into a pot, but it is the emptiness inside that makes the vessel useful. We fashion wood for a house, but it is the emptiness inside that makes it livable. We work with the substantial, but the emptiness is what we use."*

Yellow jumped on Silver's comment. "There is an old parable that goes like this…Once upon a time, there was a far-away land that was ruled by a vicious tyrant. His iron-handed rule reached into every nook and cranny of his subjects' lives—every corner, that is, except one. Try as he might, the tyrant could not destroy their belief in God. But, oh, how he wanted to. In his frustration, he finally summoned his sages and asked where he could hide God so the people would end up forgetting about him. One suggested hiding God on the dark side of the moon. This idea was debated, but was voted down because the sages feared that scientists would one day discover a way to travel into space and God would be discovered again.

"Another suggested burying God in the deepest part of the ocean. But there was the same problem with this idea, so it too was voted down. One idea after another was suggested and debated and rejected. Finally, the oldest and wisest sage had a flash of insight—'Why not hide God where no one will ever even think to look? And where would that be?' they asked. The old sage smiled and replied, 'If we hide God *inside* the people, they will never find him!'

"And so it was done. They say that even today, people in that land are still looking for God. Jon David," Yellow went on, "like the house whose emptiness shelters its inhabitants, the emptiness within you is where God resides. Go inside your emptiness—God is there."

"I'm sorry, but I just can't forget about all the suffering and evil…"

Whitie nodded her head, understanding this was a difficult notion for anyone to understand. Choosing her words carefully, she spoke softly. *"The darkness that we see in our world today is due to the disintegration of things out of harmony with God's laws. The basic conflict is not between nations, it is between two opposing beliefs. The first is that evil can be overcome by more evil, that the end justifies the means. This belief is very prevalent in our world today. It is the war way. It is the official position of every major nation. Then there is the way that was taught two thousand years ago—of overcoming evil with good…Never lose faith: God's way is bound to prevail in the end."*

Gold saw Jon David squirming in his chair, struggling to understand the concept of suffering. His aura became visibly brighter as he began to speak. *"Blessed are the poor in spirit, for theirs is the Kingdom of Heaven. Blessed are those who mourn, for they shall be comforted. Blessed are the gentle, for they shall inherit the earth.*

*Blessed are those who hunger and thirst after righteousness, for they shall be filled. Blessed are the merciful, for they shall obtain mercy. Blessed are the pure in heart, for they shall see God. Blessed are the peacemakers, for they shall be called children of God. Blessed are those who have been persecuted for righteousness' sake, for theirs is the Kingdom of Heaven."*

Jon David thought to himself, "Those words…I know I have heard those words before." Out loud he said, "But what about hate and war?"

"Every person has been given the mighty power of free will, which they can use wisely or with ignorance," added Yellow to help clarify. "God respects this earthly right. We can choose any of many dualities—love or hatred, anger or forgiveness, war or peace, fear or happiness, darkness or light. The wise among us use this power to align ourselves to God's way and find peace and happiness. Those using the power with ignorance will know only pain, fear and suffering."

Silver looked at Yellow and nodded in agreement. *"If you open yourself to the Tao, the Tao will eagerly welcome you. If you open yourself to virtue, virtue will become a part of you. If you open yourself to loss, the lost are glad to see you."*

"I guess I have set the bar pretty high for ignorance."

Silver laughed. "Jon David, we agree on one thing."

He couldn't help but laugh too. The old man had spunk.

Silver cleared his throat and continued. *"If you can empty your mind of all thoughts your heart will embrace the tranquility of peace. Watch the workings of all of creation, but contemplate their return to the source. All creatures in the universe return to the point where they began. Returning to the source is tranquility because we submit to Heaven's mandate. Returning to Heaven's mandate is called being constant. Knowing the constant is called 'enlightenment.'*

*"Not knowing the constant is the source of evil deeds because we have no roots. By knowing the constant we can accept things as they are. By accepting things as they are, we become impartial. By being impartial, we become one with Heaven. By being one with Heaven, we become one with Tao. Being one with Tao, we are no longer concerned about losing our life because we know the Tao is constant and we are one with Tao."*

Jon David nodded slowly, and then turned to Whitie. "Please tell me more about your view of God."

Whitie smiled, thought for a moment, and replied, *"Intellectually I touched God many times as truth and emotionally I touched God as love. I touched God as goodness. I touched God as kindness. It came to me that God is a creative force, a motivating power, an over-all intelligence, an ever-present, all pervading spirit—which binds everything in the universe together and gives life to everything. That brought God close. I could not be where God is not. You are within God. God is within you."*

Jon David mulled over her words. "So, how do I find enlightenment? And what happens after enlightenment?"

Silver scrunched up his face and laughed. "The enlightened Zen masters have a saying: 'Before enlightenment, chopping wood, carrying water. After enlightenment, chopping wood, carrying water.'" All of them laughed at his comment. He went on. *"Without opening your door, you can know the whole world. Without looking out your window, you can understand the way of the Tao. The more knowledge you seek, the less you will understand. The Master understands without leaving, sees clearly without looking, and accomplishes much without doing anything."*

Jon David looked down at the cabin floor, averting eye contact with the others. He spoke next in a hesitant voice "Once, I was a pretty cocky guy full of confidence. Now, I worry about everything. I seem to be afraid all the time—even afraid of the dreams in the night, afraid of what will be next, afraid of dying penniless. Worry, pain, and fear are all I have known since Iraq. That doesn't leave much room for 'enlightenment.'"

Gold listened intently and waited until Jon David's eyes met his. *"Don't be anxious for your life, what you will eat, nor yet for your body, what you will wear. Life is more than food, and the body is more than clothing. Consider the ravens: they don't sow, they don't reap, they have no warehouse or barn, and God feeds them. How much more valuable are you than birds! Isn't life more than food, and the body more than clothing? By being anxious, can [you] add one moment [to your] lifespan? Consider the lilies of the field, how they grow. They don't toil, neither do they spin, yet I tell you that even Solomon in all his glory was not dressed like one of these. But if God so clothes the grass of the field, which today exists, and tomorrow is thrown into the oven, won't he much more clothe you, you of little faith?"*

Whitie spoke in a loving way. *"How often are you worrying about the present moment? The present is usually all right. If you're worrying, you're either agonizing over the past which you should have forgotten long ago, or else you're apprehensive over the future which hasn't even come yet. We tend to skim right over the present moment which is the only moment God gives any of us to live. If you don't live the present moment, you never get around to living at all. And if you do live the present moment, you tend not to worry. For me, every moment is a new and wonderful opportunity to be of service."*

"Jon David," said Purple, "you worry about the past and you worry about the future. That leaves no time for the now, the present moment."

"What's so important about the present moment?"

"Because *life* exists there and nowhere else."

Yellow agreed with Purple's comment. "The past and future greedily beg for the tastiest morsel of all time—the present moment."

"Jon David," said Purple, "You cannot grasp the hands of the great cosmic clock and force time either backward or forward; the only portion of time that is yours to captain is the present moment."

*"Live this day!"* said Whitie. *"Yesterday is but a dream and tomorrow is only a vision, but today well lived makes every yesterday a dream of happiness and every tomorrow a vision of hope. Never agonize over the past or worry over the future. Live this day and live it well."*

Jon David nodded. "So, how do you find inner peace so you can live in the present moment?"

Silver leaned over and whispered something to Gold, who nodded in agreement. They smiled at each other, and Silver turned his attention to Jon David. *"If you want to become whole, first let yourself become broken. If you want to become straight, first let yourself become twisted. If you want to become full, first let yourself become empty. If you want to become new, first let yourself become old. Those whose desires are few gets them, those whose desires are great go astray. For this reason the Master embraces the Tao, as an example for the world to follow. Because she isn't self centered, people can see the light in her. Because she does not boast of herself, she becomes a shining example. Because she does not glorify herself, she becomes a person of merit. Because she wants nothing from the world, the world can not overcome her. When the ancient Masters said, 'If you want to become whole, then first let yourself be broken,' they weren't using empty words. All who do this will be made complete."*

"Well, I have the 'let yourself be broken' part down pretty well."

Gold bowed his head for a moment, and raised his eyes to Jon David. "I too have known pain and suffering."

"How did you cope with it?"

Gold paused in thought, searching for the right words to say. Then, the expression on his face changed to a slight smile when the words he wanted came to him. "Buddha said that on the long journey of human life, faith is the best of companions. Faith is the best refreshment on the journey and faith is the greatest treasure you will ever have. Have faith, Jon David. Have faith." He then went back to Jon David's question. "How did I cope with pain and suffering?" he said softly. "I prayed."

"How should I pray?"

*"When you pray, enter into your inner room, and having shut your door, pray to your Father who is in secret, and your Father who sees in secret will reward you openly. In praying, don't use vain repetitions, as [many] do; for they think that they will be heard for their much speaking. Therefore don't be like them, for your Father knows what things you need, before you ask him."*

Whitie smiled at Gold and added, *"The most important part of prayer is what we feel, not what we say. We spend a great deal of time telling God what we think should be done, and not enough time waiting in the stillness for God to tell us what to do."*

Purple then spoke. "Jon David, if I could move beyond the negatives of your situation, I would ask not why it is happening, but rather, what the circumstance is possibly providing—perhaps a chance to address and explore the stories of your old scars, bestowing the grace of forgiveness if merited. Or maybe the chance to discover the true essence of living which may have been neglected in the dash of the years; the chance to touch the tenderness of each moment that life presents; the chance to cry unrelenting tears to see what is washed away and what becomes uncovered; the chance to discover in the rawness of your pain any message it is telling you; the chance to embrace and heal your faltering body with gentleness and compassion; the chance to meet, in quiet stillness, the source of your being, perhaps for the first time on terms not dictated by you."

*"There will be pain in your spiritual growth,"* said Whitie. *"Until you will to do God's will and no longer need to be pushed into it. When you are out of harmony with God's will, problems come. Their purpose is to push*

*you into harmony. If you would willingly do God's will, you could avoid the problems."*

Yellow raised a hand. "And, Jon David, until you learn to forgive, the pain and suffering will never go away." The others nodded.

"Forgive whom? Do you mean forgive *them*?"

They again nodded in unison.

"I'll NEVER forgive those rat-bastards who killed my friends and those children! You can count on it!" Gold winced at the loudness and conviction of Jon David's words. He replied quietly, but firmly. *"For if you forgive men their trespasses, your heavenly Father will also forgive you. But if you don't forgive men their trespasses, neither will your Father forgive your trespasses."*

"Until you forgive, you keep your spirit in an invisible cage," Purple added.

Yellow jumped in. "Mechtild of Magdeburg said it best: *The day of my spiritual awakening was the day I saw, and knew I saw, all things in God and God in all things."*

Jon David crossed his arms and clenched his jaw; his body language did his talking—forgiveness was simply not in him.

Silver sensed his struggle. *"What is a good person but a bad person's teacher? What is a bad person but raw material for his teacher? If you fail to honor your teacher or fail to enjoy your student, you will become deluded no matter how smart you are. It is the secret of prime importance."*

Whitie smiled at Jon David. *"Concealed in every new situation we face is a spiritual lesson to be learned and a spiritual blessing for us if we learn that lesson. It is good to be tested. We grow and learn through passing tests. I look upon all my tests as good experiences. Before I was tested, I believed I would act in a loving or non-fearing way. After I was tested, I knew! Every test turned out to be an uplifting experience. And it is not important that the outcome be according to our wishes."*

"Let me get this right. Are you saying I'm being tested?"

Whitie nodded affirmatively. *"I have chosen the positive approach. I never think of myself as protesting against something, but rather as witnessing for harmonious living. Those who witness for, present solutions. Those who witness against, usually do not—they dwell on what is wrong, resorting to judgment and criticism and sometimes even name-calling. Naturally, the negative approach has a detrimental effect on the person who uses it, while the positive approach has a good effect. When an evil is attacked, the evil mobilizes, although it may have been weak and unorganized before, and therefore the attack gives it validity and strength. When there is no attack, but instead good influences are brought to bear upon the situation, not only does the evil tend to fade away, but the evildoer tends to be transformed. The positive approach inspires; the negative approach makes angry. When you make people angry, they act in accordance with their base instincts, often violently and irrationally. When you inspire people, they act in accordance with their higher instincts, sensibly and rationally. Also, anger is transient, whereas inspiration sometimes has life-long effect."*

"I never thought of it in that way. Your words offer a different perspective," Jon David said. Whitie smiled at his genuineness.

*"Don't judge, and you won't be judged,"* said Gold. *"Don't condemn, and you won't be condemned. Set free, and you will be set free."*

"Meister Eckhart said that in this life we need to become heaven so that God might find a home here," said Yellow.

Silver raised his hand slightly. *"When the Tao is used to govern the world then evil will lose its power to harm the people. Not that evil will no longer exist, but only because it has lost its power. Just as evil can lose its ability to harm, the Master shuns the use of violence."*

"Jon David," said Purple, "there is one person more than all others you need to forgive."

"Who is that?" he asked, dreading the answer he suspected was coming.

"That person is you."

Purple had struck a chord with this comment. There was a long pause before Jon David replied. He bowed his head and said, almost whispering. "I, I have killed others."

"That is why the first person you need to forgive is you."

Gold agreed, saying, *"A certain man had two sons. The younger of them said to his father, 'Father, give me my share of your property.' He divided his livelihood between them. Not many days after, the younger son gathered all of this together and traveled into a far country. There he wasted his property with riotous living. When he had spent all of it, there arose a severe famine in that country, and he began to be in need. He went and joined himself to one of the citizens of that country, and he sent him into his fields to feed pigs. He wanted to fill his belly with the husks that the pigs ate, but no one gave him any. But when he came to himself he said, 'How many hired servants of my father have bread enough to spare, and I'm dying with hunger! I will get up and go to my father, and will tell him, 'Father, I have sinned against heaven, and in your sight. I am no more worthy to be called your son. Make me as one of your hired servants.'*

"*He arose, and came to his father. But while he was still far off, his father saw him, and was moved with compassion, and ran, and fell on his neck, and kissed him. The son said to him, 'Father, I have sinned against heaven, and in your sight. I am no longer worthy to be called your son.' But the father said to his servants, 'Bring out the best robe, and put it on him. Put a ring on his hand, and shoes on his feet. Bring the fattened calf, kill it, and let us eat, and celebrate; for this, my son, was dead, and is alive again. He was lost, and is found.*"

"I never thought about forgiving myself, but you're right, it has to start with me."

Gold motioned with his arm at Silver and Purple and then spoke. "*Which of you men if you had one hundred sheep, and lost one of them, wouldn't leave the ninety-nine in the wilderness, and go after the one that was lost, until he found it? When he has found it, he carries it on his shoulders, rejoicing. When he comes home, he calls together his friends and his neighbors, saying to them, 'Rejoice with me, for I have found my sheep which was lost!' I tell you that even so there will be more joy in heaven...*"

Jon David looked down after Gold spoke, then humbly looked back at Gold and mouthed the words "thank you." His eyes brimmed with tears, as did Gold's when he gave a silent "you're welcome" in reply.

"Jon David," said Yellow, "the pain in your life has been a teacher. Only pain could bring you to where you are now. The time is now to begin your divine purpose."

# 12

"WHAT IS MY DIVINE purpose—why am I here?"

Yellow thought for a moment on how best to answer. "You, teetering on the edge, flirting with the abyss, you ask me why you are here, and I, the poet, can only reply, you are here to save the world with your smile. Jon David, no one can tell you what your divine purpose is except the still, small voice within."

Whitie added to what Yellow said. *"If you don't know what God's guidance for your life is, you might try seeking in receptive silence. I used to walk receptive and silent amidst the beauties of nature. Wonderful insights would come to me which I then put into practice in my life."*

Purple agreed. "Find your silence. The answers are there."

"Silence is a hard thing to play," said Jon David, knowing that quieting his mind was very difficult.

Whitie addressed Jon David's comment. *"The path of the seeker is full of pitfalls and temptations, and the seeker must walk it alone with God. I would recommend that you keep your feet on the ground and your thoughts at lofty heights, so that you may attract only good. Concentrate on giving so that you may open yourself to receiving; concentrate on living according to the light you have so that you may open yourself to more light; get as much light as possible through the inner way. If such receiving seems difficult, look for some inspiration from a beautiful flower or a beautiful landscape, from some beautiful music or some beautiful words. However, that which is contacted from without must be confirmed within before it is yours."*

"What is your divine purpose?"

*"My mission,"* Whitie continued, *"is to help promote peace by helping others to find inner peace. If I can find it, you can too. Peace is an*

*idea whose time has come. I have only one desire now: to do God's will for me. There is no conflict. When God guides me to walk a pilgrimage I do it gladly. When God guides me to do other things I do them just as gladly. If what I do brings criticism upon me I take it with head unbowed. If what I do brings me praise I pass it immediately along to God, for I am only the instrument through which God does the work. When God guides me to do something I am given strength, I am given supply, I am shown the way. I am given the words to speak. Whether the path is easy or hard I walk in the Light of God's love and peace and joy, and I turn to God with psalms of thanksgiving and praise. This it is to know God. And knowing God is not reserved for the great ones. It is for little folks like you and me. God is always seeking you..."*

"So, then, why are there wars?" asked Jon David.

Whitie replied quickly. *"The number one world problem is immaturity. We choose to live at a small fraction of our real potential. In our immaturity we are greedy: some grab more than their share so that others starve. In our immaturity we are fearful: we build up armaments against one another, resulting in war. If we work on world problems, we usually work at the level of symptom. I have chosen to work primarily at the level of removing cause. Knowing that all things contrary to God's laws are transient, let us avoid despair and radiate hope for a warless world. Peace is possible, for thoughts have tremendous power."*

Silver moved to the edge of his chair. *"Those who rejoice in victory delight in the slaughter of humanity. Those who resort to violence will never bring peace to the world."*

Gold added to what Silver said. *"One who is slow to anger is better than the mighty; one who rules his spirit, than he who takes a city. Blessed are the peacemakers, for they shall be called children of God."*

"Peace. It's a one-word prayer," said Purple.

"So, where is God in all of this?"

Silver took this question on. *"The great Tao flows unobstructed in every direction. All things rely on it to conceive and be born, and it does not deny even the smallest of creation. When it has accomplished great wonders, it does not claim them for itself. It nourishes infinite worlds, yet it doesn't seek to master the smallest creature. Since it is without wants and desires, it can be considered humble. All of creation seeks it for refuge yet it does not seek to master or control. Because it does not seek greatness; it is able to accomplish truly great things."*

Yellow pointed to the Igloo ice chest. "Jon David, you need both hands to hold that big chest. So it is with positive and negative. You can only hold one of them in your grasp at a time. Which one to choose is up to you, but know that the one you opt for will govern your life for as long as you hold it."

Whitie smiled at Yellow and enthusiastically added, *"If you realized how powerful your thoughts are, you would never think a defeatist or negative thought. Since we create through thought, we need to concentrate very strongly on positive thoughts. If you think you can't do something, you can't. But if you think you can, you may be surprised to discover that you can. It is important that our thoughts be constantly for the best that could happen in a situation—for the good things we would like to see happen."*

Jon David nodded in agreement. No one spoke for a while, giving him time to absorb their words.

Purple looked at the others and spoke. "Jon David, we must soon leave you."

Jon David frowned. "Please don't go—I, I have so many more questions to ask."

"You have all the knowledge you need," said Gold. "If you have any questions, you know where to go, and that is within."

They each took a turn to say one last thing to Jon David. Silver, the delightful old rascal, went first.

*"Those who know others are intelligent; those who know themselves are truly wise. Those who master others are strong; those who master themselves have true power. Those who know they have enough are truly wealthy. Those who persist will reach their goal. Remember this, Jon David, the tallest tree begins as a tiny sprout. The tallest building starts with one shovel of dirt. A journey of a thousand miles starts with a single footstep."* Silver winked and nodded at Purple to have his turn.

"Jon David, I will leave you with two thoughts to ponder. The first is a wonderful passage from the Bible:

*"If I speak with the languages of men and of angels, but don't have love, I have become sounding brass, or a clanging cymbal. If I have the gift of prophecy, and know all mysteries and all knowledge; and if I have all faith, so as to remove mountains, but don't have love, I am nothing. If I dole out all my goods to feed the poor, and if I give my body to be burned, but don't have love, it profits me nothing. Love is patient and is kind; love doesn't*

*envy. Love doesn't brag, is not proud, doesn't behave itself inappropriately, doesn't seek its own way, is not provoked, takes no account of evil; doesn't rejoice in unrighteousness, but rejoices with the truth; bears all things, believes all things, hopes all things, endures all things. Love never fails... For now we see in a mirror, dimly, but then face to face. Now I know in part, but then I will know fully, even as I was also fully known. But now faith, hope, and love remain—these three. The greatest of these is love."*

Purple waited a few moments for the words to settle and then spoke again. "Jon David, I want you to know that I am praying for you from a perspective that is spiritual. The kind of praying that surrounds you in the splendid protection of something whole, something infinitely good—something divine that I cannot, in my poverty of words, ever hope to adequately describe. But I feel its presence and know that you are part of it, part of the Oneness that lives forever and binds the universe together."

"Thank you," Jon David said, with tears freely flowing down his face.

Sporting a big smile, Yellow went next. "Oh, to be vibrantly alive and gloriously lost within an infinity of possibilities! Jon David, never forget that the world is missing what can be found in you. I will leave you with the thoughts of three enlightened people. Mahatma Gandhi said, *'In a gentle way, you can shake the world.'* Oliver Wendell Holmes had it right when he said, *'Alas for those that never sing, but die with all their music in them!'* And lastly, John Newton wrote, *'Amazing Grace, how sweet the sound, that saved a wretch like me. I once was lost but now am found, was blind, but now I see...Through many dangers, toils and snares I have already come; 'tis Grace that brought me safe thus far and Grace will lead me home...'"* Yellow raised a hand, fingers spread, and palm facing Jon David, as if radiating energy to him. "All the darkness in the world cannot put out the light of even the most humble candle. Jon David, when you find the Light within you, you will never again walk in darkness. And wherever you go, your light will shine brightly so that others may see. You have much to offer to this world my friend, much to live for—let the music within you play."

Jon David smiled through his tears and whispered "thank you" to Yellow.

Next was Whitie, the enchanting sage. She lovingly looked at Jon David, as if he were one of her own. *"I am constantly thankful. The world is so beautiful, I am thankful. I have endless energy, I am thankful. I am plugged into the source of Universal Supply, I am thankful. I am plugged into the source of Universal Truth, I am thankful. I have this constant feeling of thankfulness, which is a prayer."* She paused for a moment, smiled, and added one last thing. *"The way of peace is the way of love. Love is the greatest power on earth. It conquers all things."* She blew him a kiss with her hand.

Finally, it was Gold's turn to speak. Jon David felt a powerful affinity to him. Maybe it was because Gold was young like him. He noticed a tear rolling down the glowing figure's face as he began to speak. "Jon David," he began, trying hard to keep his voice from breaking up, *"the Kingdom of God doesn't come with observation; neither will they say, 'Look, here!' or, 'Look, there!' for behold, the Kingdom of God is within you. With God all things are possible. Peace I leave with you. My peace I give to you; not as the world gives, give I to you. Don't let your heart be troubled, neither let it be fearful."*

In a sign of love, he brought his hands to his heart, and then moved both hands away from his body, toward Jon David.

After a few moments of reflective quiet, the glowing figures moved to Jon David. They took turns hugging him and he tearfully thanked each one. After a final round of goodbyes, they departed through the cabin's front door. Gold was the last to leave. With one foot out the door, he turned around and looked at Jon David. He came back in, gave him a parting embrace, and whispered something in his ear. He smiled warmly, and then left the cabin, closing the door behind him without speaking another word.

Jon David grabbed his parka, opened the door, and stepped onto the porch to see where his friends were going. To his amazement, they were nowhere to be seen. There were no tracks in the freshly fallen snow…

He stood for a long time, eyeing the winter panorama. The only sound breaking the stillness was the noise of his teeth, which were now chattering in the subzero cold. Overhead, a brilliant aurora lit up the dark winter night. In a flash of insight, he realized where his friends had gone. They were dancing across the heavens.

# 13

HE SLEPT SOUNDLY that night for the first time in years—the kind of deep sleep that comes from being free of dragons and full of angels.

He awoke feeling...*refreshed?* But that wasn't exactly the word to describe it. Then it hit him. Pain, the archenemy that had tormented him mercilessly, was absent from duty. His body was transmitting no reports of pain! It was a new and strange feeling. He actually felt...*good?*

Without looking, Jon David reached for the medicine on the night-stand, hoping the pills would prolong this unusual feeling. His hand felt none of the plastic bottles. He swept the entire surface area to no avail. He sat up and looked at the table. A pang of alarm hit him. All the medicine bottles were gone, as was the whiskey. He stared at the nightstand, trying to make sense of things, and then surveyed the room for the missing treasures. Nothing.

He decided to get up and stoke the fire, since he could now see his breath. The cold had worked its way in. His mind was now racing—*maybe you just misplaced them, yes, that's it! All your comforts are simply downstairs.* After a few more moments, sheer panic set in. *Get moving! Find them!*

Jon David always started the morning by massaging his legs to get the one ready for the prosthetic and also to check for any shrapnel working its way out. Even his panic attack couldn't abort this ritual. As he rubbed his stump, it didn't protest with its usual sharp, stabbing pains. He shifted to the right leg and immediately noticed that his fin-gertips felt none of the shrapnel bumps that read like Braille under his skin. Unbelieving, he threw his blanket off and looked. The bumps were gone and there was only smooth skin on both legs. He stared wide-eyed in complete bewilderment. Minutes passed. The tick…tick…tick of his watch was the only sound he heard. Then, in a burst of revelation, the reason for these events dawned on him. Tears welled up in his eyes. He smiled for the first time in ages, closed his eyes, bowed his head, and said a humble "thank you."

# PART TWO

*living the message*

# 14

*Lieutenant Luke's last day in Iraq...*
*Joint Base Balad, 2100 hours*

THE FLIGHT SURGEON examined the last of the ambulatory wounded soldiers waiting to be loaded on the C-17 air ambulance. After clearing them for flight, he turned his attention to the most seriously injured soldier, who had just arrived by helicopter. The heavily sedated lieutenant was in critical condition, his body covered in a mass of red-stained bandages. Under his blanket was a void where a leg should have been. "Damn," the surgeon muttered wearily under his breath.

He motioned to a group of four airmen. They came over, lifted the lieutenant's stretcher, and walked up the rear ramp of the huge aircraft. The flight surgeon followed them into the cavernous interior. He surveyed the scene and spotted a woman who was moving from patient to patient. From her smiles and handshakes, it was obvious she was welcoming each of the wounded aboard. When her eye caught his, he motioned for her to join him. She nodded and, after a couple more hellos, came over.

"Keep a close eye on the lieutenant here, Sara. He should take the altitude changes okay, but he's already had ten units of blood. I just hope they got all the bleeders."

"Sure, Dan," she said, looking pensively at the wounded man.

"When are you heading back to the States?"

"The day after we land at Ramstein. I'll catch a hop back to Mc-Chord at three in the morning, I believe. But, on the positive side, I'll get a chance to catch some zees on the way back."

"Enjoy the green in Seattle. After being in this sandbox, I'll never complain again about rainy weather there. Tell your hubby I said hello, and I look forward to kicking his butt on the racquetball court."

"Will do," she said, laughing. "Oh! Don't email Tom that I'm coming back early—I want to surprise him."

"I won't, I promise," he said with a mischievous smile. In a few quick strides, he exited the plane, gave Sara a quick wave goodbye, and disappeared into the night.

Captain Sara Mohr turned her attention to the injured lieutenant and looked at the cardiac/physiologic monitor her team had already connected to his motionless body. There were two IVs in each of his arms for fluids and an arterial line was inserted to monitor his blood pressure. A brief look at all the tubes and monitors would convince any laymen that this was a seriously wounded soldier.

"So far, so good," she said to the attending RN. She touched the lieutenant's forehead like a mother touching her sleeping son. She looked at his file and noted his name: Jon David Luke. She leaned close to his right ear. "Rest well, Lieutenant Luke. I'll take good care of you." She looked at the flattened blanket where his left leg should have been and the bandages that covered his other extremities. Tears welled up as she put her hand on his heart, closed her eyes, and whispered, *"My dear God, please help this man."*

A critical care physician, Sara Riley Mohr headed the flight's Critical Care Air Transportation Team (CCATT), which consisted of herself, an ER-trained nurse and a respiratory therapist. Their job was to operate the aircraft's portable intensive care unit during the five-hour flight from Iraq to the Landstuhl Regional Medical Center in Germany. That day, all their efforts would focus on just one person—the critically injured lieutenant. At thirty-one years old, Sara already had an impressive list of credentials. She received a Bachelor of Science degree from Gonzaga and her MD from the University of Washington School of Medicine, then completed her residency in emergency medicine at Stanford. The daughter of an Army colonel, it was in her DNA to serve her country. She joined the Air Force Reserves shortly after completing her residency. As an Air Force captain, this was her second year leading a CCATT team. Sara quickly established herself as one of the most capable physicians in her squadron. With a constant smile and a quiet but friendly demeanor, she was known as "Sweet Sara" to all who knew her. When she wasn't deployed with the 446th Aeromedical Staging Squadron from McChord Air Force Base near Tacoma, she worked as an ER physician at the Level I adult and pediatric trauma unit at Harborview Medical Center in Seattle.

A blond with blue eyes, Sara had classic girl-next-door looks. Her five-foot seven frame was thin and taut from many miles of running each week. In the hustle and bustle of her life, running was her one pleasure. When she was twenty-eight, Sara met another runner at a half-marathon named Tom Mohr, a computer engineer. After a six-month romance, they were married. They bought a home in Redmond and settled in to a double-income, no kids existence. Both worked long hours, and with her frequent deployments, time together became ever more fleeting. Tom never complained, but she sensed his growing frustration with the demands the Air Force was putting on her. She looked forward to catching the military hop out of Ramstein to get home early.

A Humvee came roaring up to the aircraft just as it was getting ready to depart. A stern-looking Army lieutenant colonel jumped out and charged up the ramp. "Where's Lieutenant Luke?" An airman pointed to the stretcher holding the unconscious soldier. He ran over to Sara as she was reading the lieutenant's cardiac monitor. "Who are you?" he demanded.

"Sir, I'm a critical care physician."

"How's he doing?" he tersely asked, not swayed by her friendly demeanor.

"He's in very critical condition, sir. He's lost a lot of blood. We're keeping him heavily sedated."

"May I talk to him?"

"Sure. He won't respond to you, but you are welcome to try. Sir, we have to depart shortly. Every minute counts with these injured men."

"Understood."

Sara stepped out of the way. The lieutenant colonel leaned over and kissed the forehead of the stricken soldier. Tears fell from his eyes as he looked at his lieutenant's swollen and discolored face. "Jon David, this is Bergstrom. You get better, you hear?" He made the sign of the cross and said a quick, silent prayer. After another sign of the cross, he turned to Sara.

"Doctor, this is a special person you have here. Promise me you'll take good care of him."

"I will, sir, just like he was family. I promise."

"Thank you." He touched the wounded warrior's face one last time, wiped his eyes, and departed the aircraft. The huge transport's engines spooled up. Soon, it was airborne, heading to Germany.

Two hours into the flight, the lieutenant's cardiac monitor began beeping an alarm. The RN read the blood pressure and looked at Sara. "His vital signs and blood volume are dropping."

"Let's take off the blanket and see if he has a bleeder," said Sara.

When they lifted the blanket, the RN gasped. The absorbent bandage on the stump of his left leg was soaked with fresh blood. "Should I tell the pilot to head back to Balad?"

Sara looked at her watch. "No, he'll bleed out before we get back. We need to find the leak and fix it now. Prep him." She put on latex gloves and cut the sutures at the end of the stump. Blood poured out. She moved the transected flesh out of the way and spotted a hemorrhaging arterial vessel. She clamped off the blood flow, sutured a tear in the errant vessel, and released the clamp. After waiting a few moments to ensure her sutures were holding and this was the only leaker, she re-sutured the stump and bandaged it again.

"Great job, Sara. His vital signs are looking good."

"Wow, that was way too close," Sara said, letting out a sigh of relief.

Her heroics drew the attention of all the ambulatory patients on the plane. When they saw Sara take off her latex gloves as a signal that the crisis had passed, they erupted into a tsunami of clapping and cheers. Sara blushed and acknowledged the cheers. She'd just saved her patient's life. The high that coursed through her reaffirmed yet again why she loved her job and how she was born to be a healer, a preserver of life.

Sara relayed what had transpired to the Army's Landstuhl Regional Medical Center and informed them that more work would be required to repair the lieutenant's stump. Three hours later, the flight touched down at Ramstein Air Force Base. The lieutenant and the other wounded soldiers were transported by ambulance to Landstuhl. A crew bus pulled up to take Sara and her team to base quarters for some much deserved rest.

# 15

THE C-17 GENTLY touched down and taxied to a staging area. The pilot shut down its four engines, bringing an eerie quiet after many hours of constant engine roar.

"Ma'am, we're home," said a young airman as he touched Sara's shoulder. She awoke with a start. When she saw his familiar face, her mind retracted the panic alarm.

"Thanks, Johnny," she said with a yawn. "What time is it?"

"1030 on the dot, ma'am."

"Great!" she said, pleased to be getting back before noon. There would be plenty of time for her to surprise Tom. She gathered her gear, which included a Kevlar helmet and flak vest. After completing required paperwork and turning in her gear, she called a cab. Her excitement was building. She couldn't wait to be with Tom and feel his arms around her again.

The cab arrived within fifteen minutes and the driver filled Sara in on local events. When they rounded the corner on Sara's street, she was surprised to see Tom's car already in the driveway. She wondered if Dan had slipped up and spilled the beans about her coming home early. At the front door, she thanked the cabbie with a nice tip.

Sara was elated to be home. She couldn't wait to see Tom—maybe Dan was right in telling him that she'd be home early today. She opened the door and stepped in, leaving her bags outside.

"Tom, I'm home," she said with a big smile, ready for her home-coming welcome. There was no reply.

"Tom?"

She went into the kitchen. No reply.

"Tom!"

She walked down the hallway, toward the bedroom. The door was closed. She opened it.

"Tom, are you in here?"

She saw movement in their bed. He jumped up, naked, and reached for his underwear. A woman, a brunette, pulled the sheets over her naked body.

Sara gasped in disbelief.

"Sara, let me explain."

She was stunned. She felt faint and grabbed the doorway frame to steady herself.

"Sara, just wait. I, I can explain."

She looked once more at the pretty brunette lying in her spot on the bed. Their eyes met and the woman slyly smiled. She closed the door and slowly walked back to the living room.

A moment later, Tom came out, putting on his T-shirt. "Sara, I didn't know you'd be home this soon. But come on, what did you expect? You're hardly ever here and when you are, it's only to rest up so you can be gone again."

Sara couldn't speak. She pulled out her cell phone to call a cab, but its numbers were obscured by her tears.

"Sara…"

She held up her hand in a silent "stop" and moved to the front door.

"Sara, please. I don't think we ever really loved each other. Sara. Wait. Let's keep our parting civil, okay?"

*You've got to be kidding*, she thought as she stepped onto the porch and slammed the door shut. She was only half surprised that he didn't follow her. *What difference would it make anyway?*

It had started raining hard. Her mind was racing. *What am I supposed to do now? Where to go?*

She staggered to the sidewalk and started walking down the street. Her tears turned to open sobbing, blurring her vision. She felt dizzy and sat down on the first bench she came to.

In the falling rain in a neighbor's front yard, the world of Dr. Sara Riley Mohr had just turned upside down.

# 16

"MITCH, COME HERE, someone's in our yard," said the elderly woman as she looked out her living room window.

Her husband came over. "Isn't that the young lady—the doctor—from a few doors up the street, the one we met at the block party? What was her name? Lisa, I think."

"I think you're right. But her name isn't Lisa. It's Jane."

"She looks like she passed out," he said, peering over his bifocals. He stared a moment longer.

"Should I call the paramedics? The police?" the woman asked.

"Hold on a minute. Let me go see what's wrong." He grabbed a raincoat. His wife waited inside, phone at ready in her hand.

"Excuse me. Miss, excuse me…" She didn't move. He touched her arm. "Miss, are you okay?" he said in a louder voice.

She raised her head and looked at him. Even in the pouring rain, he could see she was crying.

"I, I am sorry, sir," she said between sobs. "Don't worry about me. I'll just be here a minute."

"Is there anything my wife or I can do to help you?" Rain whipped off her hair as she shook her head from side to side in a silent gesture saying no.

"My name is Mitch. Mitchell Holden. My wife over there is Pamela—Pam. I believe we met at the block party a while back. Your name is Lisa, right?"

"No sir, my name is Sara and yes, we did meet at the block party. I'm so sorry to trouble you." She stood up and felt her world go dark. She dropped back down on the bench.

That was enough for Mitch. "I'm going to have Pam call the para-medics."

"No, no, I'll be fine. I'm a doctor. I'm so sorry for bothering you."

"You're not bothering me at all. Tell you what, if you're up to it, let me help you inside so you can get dried off. Pam has soup on the stove and there's plenty to go around."

Sara was in no position to argue and nodded an okay.

A few minutes later, Mitch helped her to her feet, and together they went into the house.

"Pam, this is Sara."

"You poor thing. What on earth is wrong?" she said, handing her a towel and motioning for Sara to sit on the couch.

"Pam, maybe that isn't our business."

"You're right, Mitch. Please forgive me, Sara. Curiosity often gets the best of me." With another towel, she dabbed moisture off her face. Sara reached for Pam's hand. She told them what had happened.

"Bastard," Mitch said in summation of her story.

Pam brought the sobbing neighbor into her arms. After hugging her for a long time, she cupped Sara's face in her hands. "Dear, you need to warm up. Let's put your clothes in the dryer. I'll bring you some of my clothes to wear in the meantime. You can change in the bathroom. After that, please have lunch with us. Some hot soup is just what you need to warm up. I don't want you to catch a cold."

"Thank you so much," said Sara, who now felt drained.

After dressing, she looked in the mirror. Just a few hours earlier she had been in command of her world, saving a man's life. Now, here she was, helpless and dependent on the kindness of strangers.

She went to the kitchen. Mitch was sitting at the table reading the newspaper. Pam was at the stove, stirring soup and tending to sand-wiches cooking in a skillet. "Have a seat, dear. Tomato soup and grilled cheese sandwiches are about to be served." Sara smiled and sat next to Mitch.

"Are you a Seahawks fan?" he asked without looking up from the paper.

"I sure am. This will be their year, don't you think?"

"I agree, as long as the quarterback stays healthy." He picked up the front section and frowned. "Another four men died from an IED in Iraq. Our grandson, Ricky, is over there. He's a sergeant in the 3rd Brigade, stationed in Tikrit."

"I know the area. I worked on a few soldiers there."

"You were in Iraq?" Mitch asked, quizzically.

"Yes, sir. I'm an Air Force Reserve physician who heads a team that provides critical care to injured soldiers. We accompany airmen and soldiers on aeromedical evacuations from Iraq or Afghanistan to Germany."

"So, you're over there saving lives and come back to find your husband playing around. What a bastard."

"Mitch, no more of that. There'll be plenty of time to sort things out later. Right now, Sara needs to eat." She brought the soup and sandwiches to the table. "Okay everyone, let's dig in."

Sara was famished and finished her meal quickly. Pam smiled, pleased that she liked the meal.

"Sara," we'd be honored if you would stay the night with us. In fact, you can stay as long as you like. Consider this as our way of saying thank you for all you're doing to save the lives of our soldiers."

"Mitch is right, Sara. Please stay with us. It'll be fun to have some female company around here for a change." Mitch grunted and returned to his newspaper. "Come on, Sara, let me show you our guest room." Pam was beaming as if she were a schoolgirl having her best friend over.

Sara stayed with her new friends for a week until she found a condo near Harborview to lease. She also found a lawyer and within three months was divorced. She went back to her maiden name Riley, and proceeded to bury herself in work. It didn't take long for the phone to start ringing once word got out that she was single, but Sara would have none of it. Inside, she was still hurting. She knew the healing process would take a long time. Her coping mechanism was simply to immerse herself in her work. Between Harborview and Air Force missions, there was no time for something as frivolous as dating.

# 17

*Three years later...*

SARA HAD BECOME something of a one-trick pony since her divorce. Her entire existence centered on her job and this did nothing to mend her still-broken heart. She had always been an energetic and spirited physician with an easy smile; but lately, her smile appeared far less frequently and her once boundless energy seemed to wane by midday. She felt herself sliding into melancholy and decided to seek therapy. After a few visits, she grew to dread the probing of her soul. Plus, the interrogations weren't producing appreciable results. As she sat in the therapist's lair, her slow-burn annoyance flashed to anger.

"I've about had it with all this 'pour out your soul' crap," she grumbled. "It's yielding no results. I'm as unhappy today as my first day here."

The therapist, a woman in her 40s, answered. "Sara, you have classic physical and emotional exhaustion from all you've been through. Your life has no balance between work and play. When was the last time you did something fun just for yourself? Your life won't get better until you make tangible changes. First, you need to take time off and begin to re-explore life beyond your job. Find out what brings you joy. I recommend a sabbatical of at least six months."

"Six months! You have no idea how impossible that would be. All I need is a weekend or two off."

"Trust me, you cannot decompress in a weekend."

Sara rolled her eyes in frustration. "I'll think about it," she offered. "But I have something else I what to discuss and promise me you won't laugh, okay?"

"Sure. What's up?"

"This has been going on for months, but at first it seemed too trivial to mention to you. Now, I seem to be preoccupied with it."

"What's going on?"

"Well, for the past few months, my sleep has been disrupted by a recurring dream. It isn't really a nightmare. It involves an aeromedical evacuation from Iraq to Germany three years ago where I performed emergency surgery on a young lieutenant. He lost a leg and had a nasty bleeder that I was able to fix. I remember being embarrassed when the other wounded soldiers applauded after the operation. Although it isn't in the dream, after the mission, I came home to find my husband in bed with another woman. My question is why is it always this same dream?"

The therapist looked at the desk clock. "I'm sorry, Sara, but we need to conclude for today. There could be many meanings to this dream. It may take time to uncover the source. Let's make this the focus of our meeting next week."

Sara nodded, barely containing her frustration. She left and drove to Harborview. Another eight-hour shift awaited her. The rain on the drive to the hospital did nothing to improve her mood. Neither did the tasteless, fast-food burger she picked up along the way.

After working her shift, Sara pulled into the garage at her condo. She took the stairs to her unit, picked up the morning paper on the porch, and unlocked her front door. She went to the kitchen and turned on the coffee maker. While the coffee brewed, she went to the bedroom and exchanged her work clothes for some baggy, comfortable sweats. She poured a cup of coffee, nuked a bagel, and sat on the couch. As she perused the newspaper, the dream once more entered into her awareness.

*That young lieutenant, so injured. How is he doing now? Did he recover from his wounds?* an inner voice asked. She pondered this for a while, shrugged her shoulders, and turned to the entertainment section.

After finishing the paper and lingering on the couch for a while, Sara went back to her bedroom and put on her running suit. Though there was a slight drizzle, she felt the need to go for a run. A good run does wonders for the soul, she long ago learned. She decided to drive to Bridle Trails State Park, a 480-acre, second-growth forested park. It was crisscrossed with more than twenty-eight miles of trails. She adored this oasis in the busy city.

After two miles, Sara worked her way to an easy, sustainable pace. It was always during this time when her body seemed to go on autopilot and her mind cleared itself of petty background noise. She called this noise the chattering monkeys. When the monkeys were silent, the solution to any problem would appear. The only thoughts during this run after the monkeys quieted down were of the lieutenant. She found it odd that, of the thousands of people she had treated in her career, this one person had suddenly moved in and claimed an outpost in her head. After another mile, a quiet voice took up the cadence. *Find the lieutenant. See how he's doing. Find him. Find the lieutenant…*

Sara cranked off another mile and cooled down by walking the last mile. As she drove home, endorphins coursed through her, elevating her mood. Even with the runner's high, the voice within her continued broadcasting. *Find him. Find the lieutenant…*

Now becoming annoyed by the incessant voice inside of her, Sara took a quick shower. As the warm water danced upon her, she decided it was time to deal with this *"lieutenant thing"* once and for all. She logged on to her computer and searched through her mission notes. She found the medivac flight that had transported the lieutenant from Iraq to Germany. It was easy to remember the date—it was just before she found her husband in bed with that brunette. She frowned at that thought and beat down the mental picture of them together. She scanned the notes and found what she was looking for—the name of that young lieutenant…Jon David Luke.

She googled his name but came up with nothing useful. On a whim, she decided to call her friend, Dan, the flight surgeon who had certified the lieutenant as being able to make the flight from Iraq to Ramstein. Dan was now with the 332nd Expeditionary Medical Squadron at Ramstein. There was a nine-hour time difference, so Sara decided to get some sleep before calling. She shook her head, thinking she was crazy to pursue this, but now her curiosity was engaged.

She awoke a few hours later and, since it was still too early to call Germany, decided to go shopping for groceries. She grabbed some fast food on the way home. At ten o'clock, she picked up the phone and dialed her friend.

"Major Jordan."

"Hello, Dan, this is Sara Riley. How are you?"

"Sara! I'm doing well. Just got to work. What's up?"

"Dan, I need a favor. This might sound a little weird, but I'm chasing something down." She told him about her dream and her decision to find the lieutenant.

"Sara, are you sure you want to do this? Some of the stories involving these men don't turn out well."

"I know, but this is something I need to do. Until I get this out of my system, I'll never get a moment's peace."

"I can look up his medical record, but it won't have anything about where he is today."

"I know. I was thinking his medical record would have his next of kin. If I can get that, I might be able to track him down through his parents."

"Hold on, let me log on. What's his name again and when was he here?" After a few moments of searching, he struck pay dirt. "Got it! You got a pencil handy?"

"Shoot." She wrote down the names of the lieutenant's parents and their phone number. "Thanks so much Dan. I owe you."

She hung up the phone, went back to her computer, and typed in the area code. His parents lived in Virginia. It was way too late to call them, so she decided to turn in for the evening. Tomorrow, she'd call them from work. As she slept that night, the dream returned.

The next day, while on a break, Sara went to her office. From her address book, she retrieved the phone number of the lieutenant's parents. Feeling like an awkward schoolgirl about to talk to the parents of a new boyfriend, she took a deep breath and dialed the number.

"Hello," It was a woman's voice.

"Hello, ma'am. My name is Doctor Sara Riley. Are you the mother of a lieutenant named Jon Luke?"

There was hesitation at the other end of the line. "Is, is he okay?" A trembling voice indicated this call might be bringing ominous news.

"Oh, Mrs. Luke, I'm so sorry. There's nothing wrong. I'm calling because I'd like to speak with your son to see how he's doing. I was the head of the medical team that transported him from Iraq to Germany."

"Oh!" came a relieved reply. "Jon David is doing fine. He's out of the Army now and is on summer break from school at Georgetown. You just missed him. He left two days ago for Alaska and plans to spend his summer there."

"So, he's doing okay?"

"Oh my, yes, but he had a terrible time for a while after being wounded. We didn't think he would make it."

"I am so glad to hear he's well."

"He doesn't have a cell phone, but I can give you the number of friends he's staying with in Anchorage if you like."

"That would be wonderful. Thank you."

Jon David's mother gave Sara the information. "Dr. Riley, I want to thank you for taking care of my son. If you're ever in Roanoke, please drop by. My husband and I would love to meet you. He's a retired Army colonel and would love to talk shop with you."

"Thanks for the offer. My father is also a retired Army colonel. He and my mom live near Fort Meade, his last duty station. I think he's just now forgiving me for joining the Air Force Reserves."

"I hope you get the chance to talk to my son," said Mrs. Luke. "I'm sure he'd love to thank you for helping him. Be sure to ask what he's doing at Georgetown. I think you would approve."

Sara liked this woman. She reminded her of her mother. "Well, I'm due back on rounds, Mrs. Luke. I'll give that number a try. Thank you again for your kindness."

"You're most welcome. You take care, now."

"I will. Goodbye." She left the new number on the desk and went back to work. At noon, she returned to her office and made the call. A man with a deep voice answered.

"Spell."

"Um, hello sir, my name is Doctor Sara Riley and I'm trying to reach a person named Jon Luke. His mother gave me this number. Is he there by any chance?"

"Call me Jamie. No, he's not here. He's out at our cabin in the bush. Sorry, there's no phones out there."

She told Jamie her story and why she wanted to talk to Jon, or Jon David, as Jamie had corrected her. "Doctor Riley, you sound like a nice person. May I suggest something that might seem a bit bold?"

"Sure."

"You said you're in Seattle. Why not take an evening flight up. My wife and I would love to meet you. You can stay overnight at our home, and the following morning I'll fly you out to the cabin to meet Jon David."

"That's very kind of you, sir, but I really don't know Jon, I mean, Jon David." There was a pause.

"Doctor Riley—"

"Please, call me Sara."

"Okay, Sara. I've learned over the course of my years to trust my intuition. I think you feel the same way. Am I correct?" Another pause.

"I do."

"Well, your intuition is telling you to meet Jon David. Wait a second, please…" He moved the phone away from his face and yelled. "Penny, pick up the phone please." A moment later came the voice of a woman.

"Hello?"

"Sweetheart, I have a woman on the line named Sara Riley. She was the doctor who cared for Jon David on the flight from Iraq to Germany after he was wounded. She's been having dreams about him and her intuition is telling her to meet him. I say she should fly up from Seattle and stay with us. I'll then fly her out to the cabin to meet Jon David. What do you think?"

There was an immediate reply. "Doctor Riley, you need to listen to my husband. When can you come?"

"Please, call me Sara."

"Call me Penny, dear."

"I, I don't know if this is such a good idea."

"Keep talking to her, Penny, while I look up the next flight up here…"

"Really, sir, I—"

"Sara," said Penny, "Jamie and I are retired schoolteachers. We're used to people dropping by unannounced. Having you here would be no trouble at all. So, please trust yourself and perhaps view this as an adventure."

"Are you sure? I really don't want to impose." Sara's mind was racing. The hunt for this lieutenant started in Germany and then went to Virginia. Now she was talking to someone in Alaska. Things seemed to be happening too fast. Was she crazy?

"Sara, there are three flights leaving Seattle this evening for Anchorage. "Why don't you grab one and head on up. I prefer Alaska Airlines, of course."

Sara thought for a moment…*why not?* She told the Spells yes.

"Sara, this will be grand," said Penny.

"It sure will!" said Jamie. "We'll be around all afternoon, so give us a call and tell us what flight you'll be on. You'll love it here. There's no place on earth as beautiful as Alaska in the summertime."

"You two are hard to say no to," Sara said with a smile.

"Jon David will be thrilled to meet you, I guarantee it," Jamie said.

Sara hung up the phone feeling elated. The lieutenant's mother and now the Spells—they all seemed to be wonderful people. She looked at her calendar and frowned. Getting time off was going to be difficult. She closed the calendar and left her office.

Sara was astonished when her shift supervisor agreed to her taking a week off. She said a vacation was long overdue. Sara returned to her office and booked a 7 p.m. flight to Anchorage. She called and told the Spells, then she hurried home and began packing. This was the most spontaneous thing she'd ever done in her life. She liked the feeling.

# 18

BUTTERFLIES TOOK RESIDENCE in her stomach during the three-and-a-half-hour flight to Anchorage, letting Sara know that she wasn't a person prone to acting on impulse. This little junket was riddled with unreasoned decisions. But, she was determined to rid herself of the persistent dream, even if it meant stepping far away from the field of reason.

She gazed out the window and was rewarded with spectacular scenery—endless snow-covered mountains without a trace of human activity. She had always wanted to see Alaska and now here she was, doing something insanely removed from her normal, calculated approach to life.

As the aircraft began its descent to Anchorage's international airport, the butterflies in her stomach became as large as Alaska. Not even the magnificent scenery along Turnagain Arm and the Chugach Range could distract the butterflies. As the plane taxied to the gate, Sara began wondering why common sense had abandoned her. Other passengers, elated that the hours-long flight had ended, flipped open their seatbelt buckles and scrambled for their personal belongings.

Sara was in no hurry to join the frenzy. She sat with her belt still fastened and looked out the window one last time. With a deep breath and a sigh, she rose and moved aisle-ward. A soldier retrieved her pack and waited for her to enter the aisle. After exiting the airplane, she walked to the baggage claim area with the rest of the passengers.

A large crowd was waiting outside the security area. Several people were already in the happy embraces of loved ones. As she moved further into the welcoming crowd, she saw a man and woman coming to her with big smiles.

"Sara?" he said.

"Yes, I'm Sara. It's so nice to meet you, sir."

He opened his arms and gave her a hug. Penny followed his cue and offered a warm hug as well. "It's nice to meet you, Sara. Welcome to Alaska." Sara immediately felt relaxed around these people.

"And by the way, there'll be none of that "sir" stuff, young lady. It makes me feel a hundred and fifty. Let's get your bags and head on home. We have your room prepared. Tomorrow, I'll fly you out to the cabin to meet Jon David."

"That sounds great, Jamie."

Penny took Sara's arm in hers as they walked to the baggage claim area. Jamie led the way, about three feet in front of them. The doctor in her noticed his unnatural gait. Slight bulges in his pants above the knee were a dead giveaway. He too had lost a leg. She wondered how it had happened, but let it go at that.

Sara spotted her bag on the carousel and retrieved it. On the way back, she saw Jamie whispering something in Penny's ear. Penny was smiling and nodding enthusiastically in agreement to whatever he was saying.

"That's it, only one bag. How about you lead the way, Jamie, and I'll follow."

"Will do. The airport garage is this way." Jamie took Penny's hand and they began walking toward the exit. He opened the double door leading to the outside parking area.

"The air here is so fresh," Sara said, after a few steps. She took in a deep breath to emphasize the point.

Jamie smiled. "Wait till we get to the cabin. The air there and the scenery—it's heaven on earth."

The ride home was brief. The Spells were only fifteen minutes away from the airport. In Seattle, nothing was within fifteen minutes. Their home, located in the foothills above Anchorage, was a beautiful cedar-clad A-frame. A generous expanse of windows on the second-floor living room afforded a spectacular view of Cook Inlet and the Alaska

Range. The home's interior had a homey appearance. Sara felt comfortable right away.

Penny showed Sara to her room. It was after midnight and the sun was still out. Sara marveled that children were still outside playing. This truly was the land of the midnight sun, she thought.

"If you're up to it," Jamie asked, "how about we leave around nine tomorrow morning? I can have you at the cabin before noon."

"Sure." Her voice became hesitant. "Um, are you sure he won't mind us dropping in unannounced?"

"It will make Jon David's day," said Penny.

"You know, he was unconscious the whole flight from Iraq to Germany, so we never actually met," Sara added, her hesitancy showing.

"Sweetheart, believe me, Jon David will be honored, more than you'll ever know, to meet you," said Jamie. "I lost my leg in Viet Nam. I would've loved meeting the docs who saved my life. They made it possible for me to have a life with this wonderful woman here." He leaned over and kissed Penny on the cheek.

Sara smiled, caught up in the moment.

"Can you tell me a little about Jon David?"

"Oh, Sara, he's wonderful. Jamie and I sort of adopted him."

"Jon David is family, pure and simple," Jamie added. He paused for a moment. "Sara, I have to tell you, the first couple of years after Iraq were really tough on him. Really tough." His eyes brimmed with tears. "I'm so proud of him and how far he's come. Jon David inspires me."

"What about you? I notice you aren't wearing a ring. Are you single?" Penny asked.

Sara suddenly felt awkward. "I was married," she said softly. "But he found someone else to take my place."

"Bastard," said Jamie.

Sara smiled. "That's what a friend said too."

"Come on, old man, we'll keep this poor girl up all night jabbering."

"Right you are, my dear lady. Sara, I hope you'll sleep well. If you hear any snoring, please forgive my wife, she can't help it."

Penny playfully poked him in the ribs. He gave Sara a wink and said goodnight.

# 19

AFTER A WARM shower, Sara decided to turn in. She felt at ease in the Spell's home and quickly fell asleep in the comfortable queen-sized bed. She awoke when the morning sun shined into her eyes. She yawned, stretched, and got up to look out the window. Sunlight was dancing on the leaves of the birch trees, highlighting their beautiful deep-green color. Without a cloud in the sky, the morning gave hope for it being a beautiful day.

She nervously dressed in a light blue polo shirt and jeans. Anticipating Alaska weather to be as unpredictable as Seattle's, she added a Gortex windbreaker and another change of clothes into her backpack. She looked in the mirror again, wondering if the polo shirt was the right thing to wear. *This is so unlike me,* she thought. *I'm acting like I'm sixteen going on a date again!* The fluttering in her stomach reappeared. She shook her head. *You're simply going to say hello and get rid of those dreams of him once and for all. Stop being a teenager.* Still, despite chastising herself, the butterflies remained.

She glanced at a big clock on the living room wall and her mouth fell open. It was only 4:45 in the morning! She looked out the living room window. The sun was fully up—she could easily read a newspaper outside in the light. *Alaska is an amazing place,* she mused.

After brewing a cup of coffee and finding a bagel, she went out to the expansive porch, sat on a lounge chair, and marveled at the beauty of the Alaska Range. The air was crystal clear and smelled so fresh and pure. It was like a treat to just breathe it in. And so quiet. Modern-day Seattle was never like this. Her thoughts turned to Jon David and her recurrent dream of him. She wondered what she'd say when she met him—*Hello, I'm Sara. I saved your life. Nice to meet you.* Then what? This guy was a combat infantryman. What on earth would they have in common? The butterflies began fluttering again.

The sliding glass door opened, startling her. Out walked Jamie, clutching a big cup of coffee. He was unshaven and wearing a terry cloth robe. "Well, good morning, Sara. How'd you sleep?"

"Good morning, Jamie. I hope I didn't wake you. I slept well. I even thought I had slept in, until I saw what time it was."

Jamie laughed. "That's Alaska for you. It takes a while to get used to it being daylight most of the time." He pulled over a chair and sat next to her. "You know, in all the years I've lived here, I never stop marveling at this view."

"It is spectacular. And the air is ideal for a runner. I can't wait to get out and stretch my legs."

"Wait till I get you in the air. This is a perfect day for flying. We'll have a great view of Mount Susitna," he added, pointing to a mountain off in the distance.

The smile on Sara's face evaporated. "Jamie, I have to tell you, I'm really getting apprehensive about meeting Jon David."

Jamie smiled and took Sara's hand. "Young lady, put your mind at ease. Jon David is one of the nicest, most decent young men I have ever met. Penny and our two sons and daughter consider him to be family. Trust me on this—it will be fine." He paused for a moment. Tears came to his eyes. "Sara, Jon David and I know the horrors of war. We both have experienced deep depression and we both fought our way back to the light of day. Because of that, we share a bond. I know this man. This is why I can say that you're doing the right thing." Jamie's sincerity touched Sara. Without saying a word, she leaned over and kissed him on the cheek. He smiled and wiped his eyes. "How about we make an early go of it. Jon David is an early riser, and if we leave in the next hour, we can be at the cabin before ten. If I know him, he'll already have a salmon or two on the line."

Sara took in a deep breath. "Okay, Jamie, let's do it."

"Give me a few minutes to take a shower and rouse my sweet lady out of bed. She wants to make a picnic basket for the two of you."

Sara smiled and nodded an okay.

Ten minutes later, Penny poked her head out, said hello, and then excused herself to prepare the picnic basket. Sara wandered in shortly afterward. "Is there anything I can do to help?"

"You're welcome to take a seat and keep me company. I made some chicken and egg salad sandwiches last night. Plus, I put in the ultimate surprise for Jon David—his mom sent him a four-pack of Virgil's Microbrewed Root Beer. According to her, Jon David will sell his soul for one of Virgil's finest."

Sara laughed at the thought of a hardened soldier being a root beer aficionado. "I bet he loves animal crackers too."

Penny reached in the picnic basket. She retrieved a zip-lock plastic bag loaded with animal crackers and held it up. Sara gasped in surprise. They laughed until their sides hurt.

Jamie walked in looking refreshed. "What's all the laughing about?"

"Oh, we were just talking about Jon David's true loves—root bear and animal crackers."

"That dear son of mine is a man of simple tastes. Nothing wrong with that."

Penny handed the picnic basket to Jamie. "Enjoy the flight, Sara. Jamie is the best bush pilot around, so you'll be in good hands."

"Are you ready, young lady?"

"I sure am."

"Well then, off we go."

# 20

JAMIE DROVE SARA to Lake Hood Strip, a gravel runway adjacent to the airport where Sara had landed the day before. After conducting a pre-flight inspection of his Super Cub, he checked the fuel, oil, flight control systems, and other components of the aircraft. Satisfied all was well, he gave Sara a safety brief of what to do in case of an "unpredicted event." Then he loaded her gear and the picnic basket behind the rear seat in the tandem two-seated aircraft and motioned Sara to climb aboard. After making sure her seatbelt was fastened, he moved to the forward seat, put on his Ray-Ban Outdoorsman sunglasses, and the plane's headset. With practiced skill, Jamie started the engine and paused for a few moments to inspect the various dials that reported on the health of the aircraft. Satisfied all was well, he gave the plane some gas and began taxiing to the 2200-foot-long gravel strip. Squinting in the early morning sun, Sara reached in her pocket and pulled out a pair of sunglasses as well.

The Super Cub was soon in the air, bound for his cabin on the Talachulitna River. Jamie applied back pressure on the control stick, and the aircraft began climbing at around 60 miles per hour to the intended cruising altitude of 3000 feet. Forty-five minutes of breathtaking scenery later, they were approaching the cabin. Jamie pointed downward for Sara to view it from the air. As he flew along the riverbank, they saw a figure in the middle of the stream with a fishing pole in hand—*that must be Jon David,* she thought. Jamie made a second pass and rocked the wings. He glanced back and saw Jon David waving. He then circled over to the small grass-covered airstrip and set down without so much as a bump. Jamie pivoted around, taxied over to the tie-down point, and cut the engine. After waiting for the propeller to stop, he took off his headset and looked back at Sara.

"Welcome to my paradise," he said, beaming. He opened the door, climbed out, and then helped Sara to the ground.

"I've flown all over the world, Jamie, but this was the most thrilling flight I've ever had. The scenery is astonishing. I'll never forget it. Thank you." She gave him a hug. He sensed she was holding on a little tighter and longer than necessary.

"Sara, it will be fine. You can bank on it."

"If you say so."

"I do," he said with a laugh. "Now give me a hand with the gear, dear lady."

They started walking toward the cabin, about 500 feet away. Sara could see the former lieutenant coming to them. She looked him over as he came closer. He was tall and dressed in a green T-shirt and blue jeans. The jeans were mostly hidden by hip wader fishing boots. As he drew nearer, Sara could see how fit he appeared. To an untrained eye, he looked normal, but Sara observed the same unnatural gait as Jamie. But compared to the last time she'd seen him, he seemed the picture of health.

"Jon David!" Jamie yelled when they were a hundred feet from each other. "Good morning!"

"And good morning to you too, kind sir. What brings you here on this fine day?"

Jamie couldn't help but smile as they came to each other. "Come here, you big lug." Jon David returned his hug with equal enthusiasm.

Jamie turned to Sara. "Sara Riley, I'm honored to introduce you to the third son in my family, Jon David Luke."

Jon David looked at the attractive blond-haired woman with a puzzled expression. He offered his hand and Sara shook it timidly.

"Pleased to meet you, Sara. How did you end up in the middle of nowhere with this old pirate?"

Sara blushed. Before she could say a word, Jamie jumped in. "It's a long story, son. Let's go to the cabin and get comfortable."

As they neared the cabin, Jamie saw a couple of Penny's handmade willow branch chairs sitting on the porch. They complemented its warm, friendly atmosphere. He opened the door and looked inside. "Home sweet home away from home."

Sara entered. "My, Jamie, this place is beautiful. I'm envious."

"Ask Jon David later how I acquired this land."

There were a few moments of awkward quiet. Sara gazed at the floor, obviously nervous. Jamie broke the silence. He pointed to the chairs around the table. "Jon David and Sara, please take a seat."

Jon David looked more puzzled than ever, but honored his request without speaking a word. Sara followed his lead. She sat across from him.

"Jon David, this is Doctor Sara Riley. She was the ER doc who accompanied you on the medivac from Iraq to Germany. On the way, your leg started bleeding badly and she performed emergency surgery to save your life. She asked me if she could meet you, and I couldn't say 'yes' fast enough. Sara, before my son says a word, I just want to say thank you for making it possible for this young man to be a part of my life and my family's life." Jamie wanted to say something more, but couldn't. He choked up. Jon David sat in his chair, stunned. Sara took Jamie's hand in hers. No one spoke for a while.

"Dr. Riley," said Jon David. "I, I will never find the words to convey my gratitude for what you've done." *I cannot imagine you flying all this way just to meet me,* he thought, puzzled.

"Please, call me Sara. You're quite welcome. It makes me so happy to see how someone so horribly wounded can recover and thrive once more. You give me faith that my job makes a difference."

Her sincerity touched him. He reached over and put a hand on her hand and the other on Jamie's.

Jamie broke the silence. "Well, I'll leave you two to talk. JD, my boy, walk me back to my flying horse. See you in a while, dear Sara." She smiled and nodded.

Now alone, Sara eyed the cabin more closely. It was very cozy and appeared to be the perfect place for getting away from it all. After a few minutes, she went outside and looked around.

As they approached the aircraft, Jon David hesitantly spoke. "Jamie, do you think it's a good idea to leave her here alone?"

"Jon David, she's not alone. She's here with you."

"I, uh, I don't know what to say."

"You'll think of something, my boy. She has lots to talk about." He got back in his plane and put on his gear. Just before closing the door, he leaned out. "I'll be by tomorrow to pick Sara up." Jon David's mouth fell open. Before he could reply, Jamie had closed the door and started the engine. He quickly gave the plane some gas and moved toward the runway. He smiled and saluted Jon David as his aircraft headed down the airstrip. In a few moments, it was a speck in the air. Jon David stood looking incredulously at the plane.

# 21

SARA WAS SITTING on a porch chair, looking apprehensive, when he returned to the cabin. "Dr. Riley, I'm truly sorry, but that old goat told me, as he was taking off, that you'll be staying the night. Believe me, I had nothing to do with this."

Her eyes opened wide at the news. This had all the makings for being the longest day of her life. After an awkward pause, he added, "Do you like salmon?" She looked at him with a *say what?* expression before nodding yes. "Would you like some for lunch?"

She smiled. "Do you know of any good restaurants nearby?"

Jon David laughed. "No, but I have a world-class salmon stream right over here. Do you like to fish?"

"I tried marlin fishing once, but got horribly seasick."

"Well, I have an extra pole and I can guarantee you won't get seasick. Of course, you might get eaten by a bear, but at least you won't be nauseous."

"Bears?" she said with alarm.

"Yep, lots of them, but they tend to mind their own business—most of the time." His easy, casual confidence was putting her at ease, but she knew the butterflies would remain until she told him the reason she'd come to see him.

"Jon David, before you take me to be among the bears, may I talk to you about something that's been bothering me?"

"Sure. What's gnawing on you? Uh, no pun intended." He turned the other chair to face her, sat down, and looked at her with a quizzical expression, really curious about what she had to say.

She cleared her throat. "There's more than one reason why I'm coming to see you. This is going to sound weird, okay, so please just hear me out."

He saw the apprehensive look on her face. "Go on, Sara. I'm listening."

She cleared her throat again and hesitatingly began to speak. "I… I've treated thousands of patients since being a physician and, like Jamie said, one of them was you. I head an Air Force emergency care team and that's how I met you. We accompanied you on the medivac from Iraq to Ramstein. You were in really bad shape when they brought you aboard the aircraft and were unconscious the whole trip."

She looked straight into his eyes and continued. "Jon David, you nearly died along the way. You had an arterial bleeder in your stump. I had to open you up and stop the bleeding. Believe me, it's not the kind of operation you want to do inflight. Fortunately, you pulled through and after we landed at Ramstein, other physicians took over and cared for you at the Army hospital in Landstuhl. I never saw you again. No offense, but you were just another soldier, one of many that I've treated. To tell you the truth, I never gave you a second thought after we parted company in Ramstein."

She paused for a moment to collect her thoughts. Jon David said nothing, giving her time to find her words.

"For some reason, over the last several months, I've been having a recurring dream. The dream takes me back to that flight to Germany with you. There's nothing extraordinary about the dream—it's kind of like watching a homemade movie of the flight. But I can't stop it from repeating over and over. Anyway, the dream got me to wondering what happened to you—you know, did you survive and how are you doing. You began to crowd my thoughts, not only at night, but also during the day.

"Finally, I couldn't take it anymore. I knew I'd never find any peace until I found you. Maybe talking to you would make some sense of everything." She shook her head and looked embarrassed. "I had a friend in Ramstein look up your file, and he sent me your next of kin info. I called your mother in Virginia and she gave me Jamie's phone number. By the way, your mom is really nice. Anyway, I called Jamie, and, well, you know him. He had me convinced that I should get on a plane and come up here to see you. So, that's my story, crazy or not. I, I'm so glad to see that you survived and appear to be happy. It warms my heart."

Jon David gazed at her intently. He reached over and took her hands in his. "I was wondering why it took so long for you to come to me."

She looked at him with a puzzled expression. "What do you mean?"

"It's because of me that you're having your dreams."

"Jon David, you're not making any sense."

He paused for a moment, studied her face closely, and smiled. "Sara, I pray a lot. Not the kind of praying an eight-year-old does when making a Christmas wish list. What I do is something that is spiritual, as in, please show me the way. Some people call it meditating. It's like I'm making a divine connection. I listen to the still, small voice within. Over the last few months, the universe has been telling me that it's time to be with someone. So, I prayed for it to be true. I prayed to meet my perfect partner, my kindred spirit. And here you are. My kindred spirit has arrived."

Sara's mouth dropped open and she let go of Jon David's hands. She looked at him skeptically. "So, you're saying you had 'a higher power' put the dream in my head? Come on, Jon David. Let's keep this real, okay? I haven't known you for a half-hour and here you are declaring that you're putting dreams in my head and I'm your kindred spirit. Are you always this brazen?" She stood up to signal this absurd conversation was over.

Jon David smiled and stood up as well, ignoring what she'd said. "Sara, something extraordinary happened to me at this cabin a couple of years ago. If you permit me, I'd like to tell you about it in a little while. Right now, though, let's catch a fish for lunch."

She looked him in the eye. "If what you have to say doesn't involve me being your God-chosen one, then that's fine."

"What I have to tell you has nothing to do with you. But, after hearing what I have to say, you'll understand that you are, in fact, the one." He touched her cheek briefly, smiled, and before she could respond to the overly friendly gesture, went into the cabin.

Sara remained on the porch, trying to make sense of it all. This tall, good-looking man wasn't being overly weird or acting in any way threatening. His only oddity was being very sure of himself and in what he had to say. Only one thing was certain since she'd met him—his touch sent explosive currents racing through her.

Jon David returned with fishing waders and his arms overflowing with what seemed to be half of the cabin's contents. "Here's Penny's waders. You look like you have the same shoe size."

"Do you plan to hit the salmon with the charcoal?" Sara said as she looked at a bag of Kingsford charcoal in his arm.

"Say, there's a thought," he said with a laugh. "I want to get the grill going before we catch our lunch. This'll be ready in about twenty minutes. That should be more than enough time for us to catch a red."

"What's a red?"

"Red salmon. They're also known as sockeyes, but up here, they're called reds because of the deep red color they turn as they near their spawning grounds." Jon David got the charcoal going in the grill and grabbed the fishing pole and a tackle box. He looked at Sara and smiled. "Are you ready to go slay a salmon?"

"Lead on, Great Fisherman."

At the river, he stopped and put on sunglasses, as did she. "The full name of this river is the Talachulitna. The locals simply call it the Tal."

"So, how did Jamie come by this wonderful piece of property?"

Jon David laughed. "Believe it or not, he won it in a poker game in Viet Nam. His friend ran out of money, so, instead of cash, he wanted to bet some land he owned in Alaska. His poker mates decided that some desolate acreage in the Alaska bush was only worth ten bucks an acre. Jamie ended up winning the pot, which included thirty acres. He got this land for the equivalent of three hundred bucks. Anyway, after he came back to the states, he decided to see his winnings. His lucky hand in Viet Nam is the reason he came to Alaska and eventually met the love of his life."

"Wow, what a story. Do you mind if I ask—how did he lose his leg?"

"Mortar attack at Khe Sanh."

Jon David halted at the edge of the river. "Let me give you your first Alaska fishing lesson. Red salmon only run in rivers leading to a lake. They travel along the banks of a river as they migrate upstream on their way to the lake where they spawn. Reds tend to school up and rest in slow moving waters, which is usually where there's a deep hole. You know the reds are in because they like to jump out of the water and splash around. This morning, they were jumping like crazy." He stepped in the shallow water and offered his hand to Sara, who followed him in.

"There are several techniques to catch a salmon. I like catching them with a fly rod, but since you're a beginner, we'll use conventional gear with what they call a Russian River fly. If you're wearing polarized sunglasses, you can see them in the water."

"I'm in luck then—my shades are polarized."

"Great. Reds like to swim with their mouths opening and closing. They've been out at sea for two to three years and when they come up the rivers to spawn, they don't eat. So, you have to get the fly near their mouth. They strike because they get irritated at the fly bouncing around in their space and not because they're hungry. When you cast, start at an angle upstream and then let the fly bounce along the bottom until it comes broadside of the fish. If you feel a slight bump or hesitation, pull back on the rod to set the hook. Once you have a red on, that's when the fun will begin. They'll leap out of the water, charge upstream or downstream, you name it. Just make sure to keep tension on the line and play them until they're exhausted. Then you reel them in. Got all that?"

Sara laughed. "I think I do. Feel a bump, then yank, right?"

"Are you sure you haven't done this before?"

She smiled at him, her eyes meeting his. She liked being with this man.

They walked upstream for a while. Jon David stopped at a cut in the bank and put his hand over his sunglasses. "Look. There are about thirty of them in there. Do you see them?"

Sara stopped beside Jon David and peered in the deep hole. "Oh, my God, those fish are *huge*!"

"Lunch is as good as served," Jon David beamed as he unhooked the fly. He handed Sara the pole and pointed upstream. "Cast the fly out there and let it drift back into the hole. You'll be able to feel the lead weight as it bumps along the bottom. If you feel any hesitation, give the pole a yank."

Sara tried to follow Jon David's instructions, but the fly nearly landed on the opposite riverbank. "What did I do wrong?"

"You cast too hard. Just reel it back in and try again."

She did as he requested. Her next cast landed the fly perfectly in the stream. She let it drift downstream and into the hole. A second later, she yanked the pole. "I think I got one!" A foot-and-a-half long fish rocketed out of the water and began charging upstream.

"You got it!" Jon David whooped. "Let him run upstream as long as he wants. When he turns around and comes back toward you, reel in the line like crazy."

"Oh my God. Look at it leap in the air!"

"Okay, he's coming back to you. Start reeling in the line."

The crazed salmon sped back toward Sara and leaped up just in front of her. It then sped past her heading downstream. "Give him some line now and let him run." The salmon charged thirty feet downstream, leaping repeatedly. "Start reeling him in again, Sara!"

She frantically cranked the reel's handle. The salmon leaped out of the water several more times before losing its fight. By the time Sara reeled the fish to her, it was spent. Jon David reached out and grabbed her line. With an expert pull, he landed the fish, unhooked the fly, and held it up. "Sara, may I present the first fish you ever caught in Alaska!"

Sara felt elated. An adrenaline rush was pulsing through her. She moved to Jon David and gave him a hug. "That's one big fish!" she said, jubilant and beaming as she gawked at the huge red-tinged salmon. She looked at Jon David, and before she could stop herself, impulsively kissed him. For the rest of her days, Sara Riley would remember this as the exact moment she fell in love with Jon David Luke.

# 22

HE SMILED AND LOOKED into her eyes. "Are you up for having your first fish for lunch?"

"That would be wonderful. I'm famished."

"Tell you what—how about you go back to the cabin and slice up a lemon. There's one in the Igloo chest. While you're doing that, I'll clean and fillet this exceptional specimen."

"Okay." She started wading across the river, stopped, and went back to Jon David. She kissed him again. "Thank you for making this a very special day for me." Her blue eyes sparkled as she spoke. Before he could reply, she kissed him quickly once more, spun around, and crossed the river.

Back at the cabin, she remembered the four-pack of Virgil's root beer in the picnic basket. She grabbed it and ran back to the river. "Jon David, here's the surprise that needs to be chilled. She held the root beer up in the air.

"Virgil's root beer?" he said with eyes wide open. "How did you know?"

"Your mother sent them to Penny as a gift for you. I'm just the bearer of gifts."

"I do think this'll go down as the absolute best day of my life!" He came over and took the treasures from her. "The cold water will chill them quickly." He carefully placed each bottle in the clear water. "God bless you, Mom. God bless you!" Sara smiled and hurried back to the cabin. He soon followed with the filleted fish.

"You are in for a treat. The main course will be lemon dill salmon."

"It sounds delicious."

He put the salmon on a plate, grabbed a box of aluminum foil and cut two foot-long sheets, placing a fillet on each piece. Next, he went to the cooler and pulled out some carrots and a zucchini. "If you would, please slice these into thin diagonal pieces."

While she prepared the vegetables, he took a stick of butter out of the cooler, sliced it into several one-teaspoon pats, and placed them on the fillets. Next, he added the lemon slices along with the veggies that Sara had prepared. Lastly, he sprinkled on some dried dill weed and lemon pepper. He brought up the sides of the foil and double folded it to form a packet that had enough room for heat to circulate inside. "Okay, let's put these on the grill. In about ten minutes, we'll have a feast."

"Penny packed potato salad in the picnic basket. I think that would work well with the fish, don't you?"

"It sure will. That and the root beer."

"I see you are a man of simple tastes."

"That I am." He went out and placed the salmon on the grill.

Sara popped her head out. "How about eating outside—it's such a lovely day."

"You're reading my mind. Are you up for a root beer?"

"I sure am."

He went to the river and pulled out a couple of brews. They were cold to the touch. He carried the bottles like they were a rare vintage of Dom Pérignon. He handed one to Sara and then opened the other for himself. "I propose a toast." Sara raised her bottle. He paused for a moment, searching for the perfect words.

"Once, I was far from Eden, but just look at me today. This feels like heaven to me. Here's to you and me, Sara, and the beginning of something very special."

"I'll drink to that."

He touched his bottle to hers, took a swig, and raised it high. "And here's to Virgil for your amazing root beer!"

Sara took a sip and her eyes went wide open. "Oh, this is fabulous!"

Jon David smiled at her response. "Let's see if lunch is ready." He cracked open one of the foil pouches. After flicking the salmon with a fork, he looked at Sara. "Let's eat!"

She brought plates over and he opened the pouches, placing the contents on them. "Jon David, it smells heavenly."

"Just wait until you taste it." Before heading back to the porch, he put the foil on the coals to burn off the smell. In bear country, smells were like ringing the dinner bell.

Sara took a bite. "This is splendid!" She took another bite and rolled her eyes. "I'm in heaven."

"I'm glad you like it." He bowed his head and said a quick, silent prayer. He tasted it and smiled. "It doesn't get any fresher than this."

As they ate their meal, the conversation came with a light easiness. Sara was amazed at how comfortable she felt with this man who had been a stranger just that morning. Jon David couldn't take his eyes off the soft-voiced woman who had captured his heart at first sight.

"Would you like to go for a walk?" he asked after their meal settled. "There's a knoll not far from here with incredible views."

"That's a wonderful idea. I'd love to stretch my legs."

"Give me a second. I need to grab a little protection." He went inside and returned with a pistol strapped to his side.

"Do you really need that?"

"Sara, we're in the Bush in Alaska, and anything can happen. You have to respect it, but not fear it."

"You really aren't afraid?"

"I fear nothing."

"There's that cockiness again. Are you always like that?"

"Sara, earlier in my life I was what you call cocky. Now, I'm very confident. There's a big difference."

"How so?"

"Like I said this morning, I have something to tell you. I'll explain the difference then. Fair enough?"

"I'll count on that." Her soft curves molded to the contours of his body as they walked. "Hey, when I called your mom, she said you were on break from Georgetown. What's your major?"

"I just finished my first year of med school."

"You're kidding! Seriously? Have you thought about a particular specialty?"

"Yes. I love kids, so I plan on being a pediatrician. I want to help disadvantaged children around the world. Heck, I could spend a lifetime in Alaska helping Native children in the remote villages. Did you know that fetal alcohol syndrome is rampant up here?"

Sara saw the sincerity and conviction in his eyes. There were more dimensions to Jon David Luke than being a former gun-toting Army Ranger.

After climbing on a game trail for twenty minutes, they reached the top of the knoll. Mount McKinley and Mount Foraker filled the vista—a spectacular sight in the cloudless sky. "Foraker is on the left. It's 17,400 feet high—the fourth highest peak in the United States. McKinley, or Denali as we call it in Alaska, is the tallest mountain in North America at 20,320 feet."

"Wouldn't it be wonderful to have a home right here?"

"Sure, but it would be a heck of a trip to the nearest grocery store, especially in the winter. It can get to fifty below. I love winters though, once the cabin is toasty warm, that is." He wrapped his arms around her. After placing a feathery kiss on her cheek, his lips gently met hers. She quivered at the sweet tenderness of his kiss.

"Jon David, you know how to kiss a woman."

His eyes met hers and he smiled. He kissed her again, this time deeply. "You probably don't want to hear this, but I've already fallen in love with you."

"Let's not rush this, okay? You're in medical school and I live on the other coast. The chance of this working is slim, at best."

He smiled. "Say what you want, but your kisses agree with me. Besides, you're powerless to stop our love from happening. Remember, God brought you to me."

"Ah yes, your prayers. And, the mysteries you want to explain to me later."

"It was something extraordinary, Sara. Something quite extraordinary. Again, once I tell you, you'll understand everything. All I ask is that you be open to what I have to say and trust what your heart tells you."

"Well, you have my curiosity up. Do you want to head back so you can tell me your story?"

"Sure. I'll take you back on a different trail so you can see Mount Spurr. It's an active volcano that erupted not that long ago."

"Okay. Since you have my curiosity running in hyper-drive, may I ask you a question?"

"Sure. Ask away."

"Why do you go by your first and middle name?"

"Well, according to my parents, when I learned my name at the tender age of two, I insisted on being called Jon David. If someone called me Jon, I would stomp my foot and give them a ration of toddler hell. After a while, being called by my first and middle name stuck. So, the genesis of being called Jon David comes from the dictates of a tyrannical two-year-old."

"I bet your parents were relieved that you didn't insist on being called *King Jon*."

He laughed heartedly. "You know, back in my Army days, I was known as Cool Hand Luke."

"You're still pretty cool, Jon David."

# 23

THEY RETURNED TO the cabin and Sara excused herself to use the outdoor facility Jon David called *"the thunderbox."* While she was gone, he went inside and headed to the loft. He changed into a pair of shorts and a fresh T-shirt. Downstairs, he took two of Penny's willow chairs and brought them to the center of the cabin, facing each other.

Sara came in looking radiant. She had a natural peaches-and-cream wholesomeness about her, he decided. She smiled and looked a bit puzzled when she saw the two chairs in the middle of the room.

"Please have a seat," he said, pointing to one of the chairs. She took a seat without saying a word. Jon David sat down and gazed at her. He suddenly looked vulnerable, as if all his confidence had evaporated. "Sara, this is…this is really hard to talk about…"

She touched his hand and looked at him with empathy. "Take your time. We have all night."

"Thank you." Tears welled up in his eyes. He leaned back and took in a deep breath. He looked at Sara for a few moments and then began his story…

"I lost nearly everything in Iraq. Four of my men, and several kids who were following me, were killed in the attack. After I came back to the States, I started having dreams about that awful day, wicked dreams. The word 'nightmare' isn't adequate to describe them. I'd wake up gasping for air. The recurring image of a dead little boy, named Haady, looking me in the eye, shook me right down to my soul."

He paused for a moment as if reliving the nightmare.

"At Walter Reed, my girlfriend came to visit and saw this." He pointed to his stump. "She went home and promptly sent me a 'Dear

Jon' letter. That added to my rapid descent into a deep and dark abyss. I became very angry and did a wonderful job of pitying myself. Unfortunately, my dear parents and brother Danny took the brunt of my frustrations. I treated them like crap, Sara, like crap. My friends, too."

Tears flowed down his cheeks. She couldn't contain her tears after seeing his profound sadness.

"Sara, the physical pain was unbearable. I started drinking heavily. Between the pain, the endless pills, the nightmares, and the booze, my life descended deeper into the dark hole. One night I sat in my apartment and held a pistol to my head. I started squeezing the trigger, but stopped when I thought of how it would affect my parents. Dying is one thing, but suicide would break their hearts."

He closed his eyes, needing to go deep inside of himself to gather more strength to continue. Sara leaned over and kissed his forehead. He opened his eyes, looking at her like a frightened little boy.

With obvious distress, he continued the story. "The morning after putting the pistol to my head, I decided to end my life, but I knew I'd have to find a way to make it appear like an accident. That very day, I went to Walter Reed to get my pain prescriptions renewed. While I was waiting to see the doc, an obnoxious man came in and sat next to me. Much to my dismay, he wouldn't stop talking. But, then I found myself kind of liking him. He had also lost a leg. Out of the blue, he invites me to visit him in Alaska. Yes, it was Jamie. He and Penny were in DC on vacation. Well, that's what he told me then. Anyway, he gave me his phone number. I'd been stationed at Fort Richardson on my first tour of duty, and it hit me that Alaska might be the perfect place to stage an accident. I called Jamie the next day and accepted his invitation. I then went to Virginia to see my parents and kid brother, and told them I was going to see some friends in Alaska. I just needed some time to myself—an adventure, I'd called it. Little did they know that I was seeing them to say my last goodbyes."

Jon David stopped for a minute and gazed at the ceiling, trying to keep the tears at bay. He turned his gaze back to Sara. "I came to Alaska in the middle of winter. After a few days at the Spells' home, Jamie flew me to this cabin and showed me the ropes. Believe me, at 30 below, that cast iron stove over there becomes your friend. Anyway, on the first trip here, I figured out the perfect way to check out of this sorry world." He looked again at the cast iron stove. "When Jamie showed me how to use it, I remembered my Army training about never having charcoal grills inside your field tent because it would cause dangerous levels of carbon monoxide to build up. From that came an epiphany—use the stove to put carbon monoxide into the cabin. Doing so would be simple. Close the damper on the stove and open the fire door. Stay outside and let the gas rise to lethal levels. Go back in, open the damper and close the firebox door to make everything look normal. Then go upstairs and sleep, never to wake up again."

"Oh, Jon David! I can only imagine how hard your life must've been."

He was openly weeping now. Sara went over and sat on his lap. She held him tightly. After several minutes, he regained his composure and looked at her again. "Sara, I need to tell you the whole story. Please sit back down and hear me out."

She kissed his forehead and complied.

"What I have to tell you is a miracle…"

# 24

JON DAVID TOOK his time telling her what had transpired that night at the cabin. He left out no details. It was still as fresh in his mind as if it had happened yesterday. Despite the sincerity of his words and the conviction in his voice, he didn't expect her to believe him—spirits and a miraculous recovery? But deep down, a part of him hoped she would. Sara didn't say a word for a while. Then she spoke...

"Are you sure it wasn't just a dream?"

"Yes, I'm sure and I can prove it." He stood up and lifted up the right leg of his shorts. "Remember I said I'd woken up the next morning feeling no pain? Sara, it was the first time in two years that I'd felt no pain. I reached down and felt my legs. All the bumps from the embedded shrapnel were gone. Look at my leg. It used to be scarred and looked like a rough road. You, more than anyone, know how chewed up I was. Now look. Not a single scar. And Sara, since that morning, I haven't taken a pain pill or a drink."

Sara touched his leg, amazed at what she saw. She looked up at him and nodded her head in concurrence.

"That's only part of the story. For many months, Jamie kept having a dream that someone needed rescuing. It was a vague dream, but one evening when he was watching the news about wounded soldiers at Walter Reed, he knew he was supposed to go there. He told Penny, and without hesitation they flew to DC. He went to Walter Reed and started walking the halls. When he saw me sitting in a waiting area, he said he knew I was the one he was supposed to rescue. *He knew it.*"

Sara's mouth dropped open at what he'd said.

"Jamie, too, had been haunted by the horrors of war, and, like me, he had fallen into the abyss. His escape from reality took him more and more to this cabin where he drank his life almost to oblivion. At his lowest point, the sages visited him in the middle of the night right here in this cabin. So, he knew that once he got me to come to Alaska, he had to get me here."

Jon David looked deeply into Sara's eyes. "I hope you can now see why Jamie and I share an unbreakable bond. Sara, he saved my life. Can you imagine—he and Penny flew all the way to DC only on a notion that a life needed to be saved." Tears again flowed freely down his cheeks.

Sara looked at him, her eyes ablaze in marvel. "My God," she said softly. "My dear God."

"And so you see, Sara, you didn't start having your dreams by chance. It was God speaking to you. It was God putting us together."

"I believe you, I truly do." She looked at him and then bowed her head. "I wish I could talk to the spirit people, too. I, I've yet to recover from having my heart broken."

"What happened, Sara? Please tell me." It was now Sara's turn to let her heart speak. She described what had happened after she left him in Germany—how she had found her husband in bed with another woman and the subsequent divorce.

"Bastard," Jon David said in a terse voice.

Sara laughed. "Everyone says that when I tell them my story."

He kissed her forehead and looked at her with empathy in his eyes. "Sara, the sages told me that everything happens for a reason. Pain can be an effective teacher to make you act or learn a lesson. All your sorrows and joys—everything that has happened to you—collaborated to bring you here. It's the same with me."

She smiled, but couldn't fully accept his words. "I don't know if I can ever trust anyone again." Her voice was barely audible. "And, I must not have been a very good wife. I didn't give him what a man needs."

"Sara, we've both had more than our share of dark nights of the soul."

"Yes," she said, wiping her tears, "but, it's okay. I'm a pretty tough woman."

"Don't kid a kidder, Sara."

She laughed. "Okay, maybe I'm not all that tough."

He smiled and kissed her. "Sara, this cabin is a holy place. I'm convinced of it. And in this holy place, I joyfully make this vow. You will never, ever have a reason to doubt or mistrust me. I swear this to you before God."

"Really?"

He cupped her face in his hands. "As God is my witness, my dear Sara, I promise."

She looked into his eyes. "There's something else. I…" She took a deep breath. "I don't think I can be a doctor anymore. I've seen too much. A counselor said I have compassion fatigue. She was right. I have nothing more to give. That might include being able to love anyone again."

He nodded. "One of the wise people in this very spot said, to find the answer you are seeking, you have to look inside. I can only suggest you take some time off and be alone. Listen to the still, small voice within. Earlier I told you there was a big difference between being cocky and being confident. I'm confident because I listen to my inner self. When I follow that voice within, I know I'm on the right path. In my youth, my cockiness was based on nothing more than arrogant bravado. I hope you see the difference between the two."

"Are things really that cut-and-dry for you now?"

"Yes, Sara, they are. I'm on the right path when I'm happy. When I'm not, I take the necessary steps to get back on the path. It's not always easy, but I stay with it. And the only path that brings happiness is the one that includes God. Truly, God is with me at all times. I only have to take the time to listen. It's as simple as that. But, most of us have a hundred thoughts in our head at any moment. I've learned I have to quiet my mind in order to hear. Now I understand the value of meditation."

"You are a wise man, dear sir."

Jon David let out a hearty laugh. "God still needs to send down an occasional lightning bolt to my duff to get my attention."

Sara couldn't help but laugh at the mental picture of lightning bolts zapping his rear.

"Sara, take all the time you need to decide what is right for you. I'll wait for you as long as it takes. Just know that I have no doubt in my mind that you and I are supposed to be together. When you feel the same, come to me." He paused and touched her cheek. "We've covered a lot of territory and it's getting late. Why don't we call it a day and turn in. I'll make you a bed down here."

"Okay. You're right. I'm exhausted."

"I usually go down to the river to brush my teeth and wash my face. You're welcome to tag along."

"Thanks, I will. I've been told there are bears about, so, for that reason, I'll follow you anywhere."

"I knew God put bears on this earth for a reason."

She rolled her eyes and gave him another hug. "Thank you, Jon David."

"Thank you too, Sara."

They walked to the river and used the finest water in the world to wash up. On the way back, Sara stopped and looked at Jon David. "So, what was the word the gold figure whispered in your ear?"

"What do you think it was?"

"Love. It had to be love."

"No."

"Hope?" He shook his head.

"Come on, spill the beans."

"Actually, the word is just two little letters..."

Sara shrugged her shoulders. "I haven't the foggiest idea what it is now."

"The word he whispered to me was '*be.*' It's a simple word, but I've come to know the amazing power of it. I can't tell you how many times I've repeated it to myself when I'm feeling uptight, or when I'm angry over some petty thing. It calms me down and gets me centered again. *Be,* I tell myself. *Just be.* You're welcome to use it too."

"Thank you. I think I might. *Be.* It does have a humble eloquence."

They lingered a while outside, enjoying the pristine air.

Jon David made sure Sara was cozy on the downstairs air mattress, kissed her goodnight, and went to the loft.

# 25

AFTER TOSSING AND TURNING for a couple of hours, he drifted off to sleep. It took every ounce of his resolve not to go down and bring that beautiful woman to his bed. He ached to be near her.

Downstairs, Sara's battle for sleep was even more futile. With every bit of her being, she willed that amazing man to come to her and be with her forever. Never in her life had she bared her soul to another person like she'd done this night, and never had another man bared his soul to her.

Finally, Sara could take it no longer. She got up and quietly climbed the stairs. She stood by his bedside and looked at him for several moments, watching his bare chest rise and fall in rhythmic breathing. In the twilight, she noticed he was wearing a necklace with a simple gold cross. He appeared completely at peace as he slept.

She took off the large T-shirt he'd offered earlier as a sleeping gown and eased into the bed. She kissed him on the cheek and molded her body next to his. His naked warmth felt tantalizing in the cool night air.

"I was hoping you'd come to me," he whispered.

"It's been a long time since I've been with a man."

"Sara, I haven't been with a woman since before my Iraq tour." He turned and faced her. "You don't snore, do you?"

She wrinkled her nose and playfully poked his ribs. Then she turned serious. "I, I want you to know something. I'm not very good in bed. My former husband was the only man I ever slept with. He said lousy sex was one reason why he left me."

Jon David took her hand and gently placed it on what was left of his leg. He spoke in almost a whisper. "The truth is, I'm not the man I once was."

"Jon David, you're no less of a man than you were before your wounds. That will never be an issue with me."

"Thank you. Hearing you say that means a lot. And just for the record, I'm not your former husband. I promise you this—I'm willing to have sex with you every day so you can become an accomplished lover."

"You are soooo bad."

He touched his lips to hers, giving her a kiss as tender and light as a soft summer breeze. He wrapped his arms around her and looked into her eyes. "I love you, Sara. My heart is yours."

"I love you too, Jon David. I give you my heart. Please don't break it."

She kissed him slowly, lingering, and savoring every moment. He responded with a tighter embrace. His strength was exhilarating. He gently rolled her to her back and moved on top of her, kissing her again, this time with a sense of urgency. She responded, giving herself freely to the passion of his kiss.

"Sara, may I make love to you…?"

"Yes, my love, yes."

An hour passed, then two. They lay together, totally spent.

"You're an incredible lover. Words cannot describe how I feel about you. I hope you know that," Jon David said.

She was too emotion-choked to respond. The way she looked at him told him all he needed to know. She curled into the curve of his body. A deep feeling of peace swept over her. After a while, she spoke. "I'm yours forever, Jon David Luke, forever. I swear this to you now."

He kissed her once more. They lay in splendid silence.

Then Sara moved on top of him and looked deeply into his eyes. "I've had sex before, but for the first time in my life, someone has made love to me. It was the most incredible thing I've ever experienced."

"I feel the same way, Sara. You're an amazing lover. Amazing."

She smiled and suddenly looked like a frightened little girl. "May I…may I ask you something?"

"Of course you can."

"Jon David," she said, her voice quivering. "Will you marry me?"

He looked at her and furrowed his brow. "Sara, don't you think you should take some time to be with your thoughts and listen to the voice within you before asking me to marry you?"

"After you left me downstairs, a voice spoke to me, and it wasn't a still, small voice. This voice sounded like a megaphone booming within me, saying, *'Your man is up in the loft. Go be with him forever.'*"

"Are you sure it wasn't just a bad case of gas?"

"You are so bad, Mr. Luke, bad to the bone."

She turned serious again. "Will you, Jon David? Will you marry me?"

"I'd be honored to be your husband."

Tears flooded her eyes then. It was as if every emotion she'd ever experienced—the past pain, the current pleasure—all of it was released. The tears seemed to sweep away the old hurts. Jon David cried along with her, his emotions filled with the hope of bright new days ahead.

After their tears subsided, Jon David quietly spoke. "Sara, with your permission, I'd like Jamie to marry us."

"Oh, that would be such an honor. But, is he a minister?"

"In Alaska, anyone can perform a marriage ceremony if you get a temporary marriage commissioner appointment from the state. It's done quite a lot up here."

"Then it's settled. Jamie is our man."

"Thank you, Sara."

"When do you want to get married?"

"How about this Sunday?

She gasped. "Are you serious?"

"I sure am. You're the one, Sara, I have no doubt. And since there is no doubt, I can't bear to have another day go by without you being my wife."

"I have no doubt either. Sunday it is."

For the rest of the night, they held tightly to each other. They would make love twice more before morning came.

# 26

THEY SLEPT PAST ten. He awoke first and, after watching the peaceful sleep of the beautiful woman beside him, quietly got up and dressed. Once downstairs, he opened the cabin door, stepped out on the porch, and breathed in the fresh air. It felt wonderful to be alive. He closed his eyes and faced the morning sun, letting its rays warm his face. He couldn't imagine any man on earth being happier than he was now. After soaking in the sun's rays, he went to the river and washed up.

He began walking back to the cabin. Sara was on the porch, looking his way with a big smile. "Good morning, Jon David."

"Hello there, my love."

She greeted him with a big hug. "Do you still love me as much this morning as you did last night?"

"Hmmm…let me think…yes, my sweet Sara. I've never been happier in my life. How about you?"

"I've met the most wonderful man in the world. He's an incredible lover, too." She kissed him tenderly and gave him another hug. "I'll never grow tired of your embrace."

Her words made him hold her even tighter. He kissed her again and smiled. "Hey, are you as hungry as I am?"

"I sure am. We have sandwiches Penny made for us."

"Great idea. And, there are still two of Virgil's finest in the river."

"I'll get the sandwiches if you get the brewskies."

"Deal."

They sat on the porch, enjoying their meal under the glorious morning sun. They had just finished their breakfast when they heard an approaching aircraft.

"Is that Jamie already?" said Sara, her voice sounding sad. Surely he wouldn't be coming so soon. She wished for this time with Jon David to never end.

Jon David squinted as he looked at the aircraft silhouetted against the bright sun. "It's not a Super Cub. It looks more like a Cessna."

The aircraft dropped in elevation as it drew nearer. When it approached the cabin, it was only a hundred feet in the air. The pilot rocked the plane's wings as it passed overhead. It was definitely a Cessna, probably a 170 model, given its taildragger landing gear. The pilot circled back and came in for a landing on the airstrip. Jon David and Sara walked to the runway to greet whoever was in the plane. She kissed his cheek as they went and put her arm around him.

As the aircraft taxied to the tie-down area, Jon David could see two figures inside the plane. It *was* Jamie and Penny. Both were smiling and waving. He waved back.

"Hey you two. Where'd you get the plane?"

"The Okerlunds let us use it so Penny could fly with me. It looks like you and Sara got along okay," Jamie said with a sly smile.

"Well, as a matter of fact, we did. So good that we're getting married," Jon David said, beaming.

Jamie let out a whoop and raised his hands in the air. "Yes! Thank you, Lord. From the moment I laid eyes on Sara, I knew this was going to happen. I told Penny right there in the airport."

Penny laughed. "It's true. He did, and I agreed with him."

"So, that's what you two were whispering about while I was getting my bag."

"It sure was, sweetheart" Jamie said. "So, how long did it take him to propose?"

"He didn't propose. I did."

"Well, if that doesn't beat all," Jamie laughed. "Sara, I think you'll fit in perfectly with our family."

Jon David grinned when Sara broke the news of who proposed. "We want to get married this Sunday, and Jamie, we want you to marry us."

"Yes," said Sara, "we'd be honored to be married by you."

Jamie's eyes opened wide at their request. His bottom lip quivered. All he could do was nod a silent yes. Penny beamed. Jamie gave Jon David a lengthy hug as if he had waited a long time for this day to come. Finally, he regained his composure enough to speak. "I welcome you with all my heart to the family, Sara. You've made me the happiest father in the world today."

"Sara, I feel the same as my husband. I hope you and Jon David will be very happy."

"Thank you both. You've made me feel so welcome."

Penny took Sara's hands in hers. "This old man was convinced you two couldn't be together for more than a couple of minutes without falling in love. After Jamie flew home, he couldn't sit still all day. Finally, he came to me and said, *'Penny, they're going to get married, and knowing Jon David, it will be very soon.'* We spent the rest of the evening discussing the perfect place for the ceremony."

"And did you agree on where it should be?" asked Jon David.

"We sure did," said Jamie. "In Girdwood, at Our Lady of the Snows Chapel."

"Sara, it's a beautiful chapel. It's about forty-five minutes from Anchorage in the mountains. The views from the chapel are spectacular."

"It sounds wonderful, Penny. I can't wait to see it."

They spent an hour at the cabin before heading back to Anchorage. Penny wanted to bring home a couple of salmon. Jon David and Jamie quickly filled her order.

# 27

ON THE FLIGHT back, they flew over the broad Matanuska-Susitna Valley. From this vantage point, Jamie pointed out the Talkeetna Mountains to the north, and the beautiful, glacier-carved Chugach Mountains to the east. They passed so close to Pioneer Peak that Sara thought she could reach out and touch it. From there, they flew south along the front range of the Chugach, on the way to the Birchwood airport north of Anchorage.

He eased the plane to the ground and taxied to the slot where the Okerlands kept their plane. Sara gave her pilot a hug. "Jamie, I can easily see why you all love it here. Nothing is as beautiful as Alaska."

"We thank God every day for being here, although our prayers of thanks get a little shorter in February." She laughed. After securing the aircraft, they walked to the Spells' SUV, and left the small airport, bound for home.

Penny made lunch while Jon David and Sara got settled in. After a round of showers, they came to the kitchen looking refreshed. As they sat at the kitchen table, they couldn't take their eyes off each other.

"I have ham and turkey sandwiches, potato salad, chips and sodas," said Penny. "And of course animal crackers for our men."

"Jon David, it took years for me to train my wife to be so accommodating. I can pass on all my hard-won tips to you if you wish." Penny playfully poked her husband in the ribs.

"I'd like that. Do you mind if I take notes?" Sara rolled her eyes.

"So, what's the plan for today?" said Jamie. "We can show you pictures of the chapel if you like."

Penny followed up on her husband's comment. "Sara, there are a couple of nice stores that sell wedding dresses. If you choose to go that route, we can go shopping."

The thought of wedding gown shopping suddenly stopped her cold. *A wedding gown? Getting married?* "Penny, I've yet to wrap my brain around all of this. I think I need some time to digest it."

Jon David took her hand. "Are you having second thoughts about getting married?" he asked. "If so, I understand. We can wait until it's right for you."

"Not at all. Don't think you're getting off the hook that easily, Mr. Luke. What I mean is that I haven't grasped the enormity of the logistics necessary to pull this off. I have to call my parents and then get cleared for having time off from work, and all the shopping needed. And maybe a honeymoon. Then, after we're married, what will we do? I have a condo and will need to move to be with you. Wow. I feel overwhelmed just talking about it."

"Young lady, my advice is don't try to eat the elephant whole. Take a bite at a time. As schoolteachers, Penny and I know a thing or two about organization. Let us work with you to make it happen. We can handle things like booking the chapel and picking people up from the airport. There's enough room for your parents to stay here if they choose. We're family and we stand ready to assist you."

Sara didn't say a thing. She simply leaned over and kissed his cheek. Jamie put his hand on hers. He found her reply to be more than an adequate "thank you."

"Sara, I need to ask your father for your hand. You might want to talk to your parents first, so my calling won't hit them like a bolt out of the blue."

"Trust me, Jon David, no matter if I call them, it'll be a bolt out of the blue. A big bolt. I'll call them after lunch."

"Do you mind me calling my parents first? It'll help me get prepared for telling our story to your dad. By the way, is he nice?"

Sara laughed. "He's a retired Army colonel who eats lieutenants like they were sardines."

"Uh, oh. I never much got along with higher ups. They accused me of being cocky. Can you believe that?"

Sara almost choked on her soda with his remark. "You, cocky? Why, I never would've guessed."

Following lunch, Jon David excused himself to the deck to call his parents. After the shock factor of his wedding announcement subsided, if he had kept count, the words "are you sure" and "why not wait and get to know her better" came up about forty times. In the end, they accepted his decision, but only after he told them what happened at the cabin with Sara. They long ago accepted what transpired there and how it transformed their son's life. If Spirit was continuing to manifest in their son, who were they to argue? They asked to speak to Sara. After another round of "are you sure" and "why not wait and get to know him better," she had their blessing.

The call by Sara to her parents was a disaster. They could not be swayed. In tears, she handed the phone to Jon David. He stepped out on the deck to speak to her father.

"Sir, I know the brevity of our relationship makes our wedding sound like folly, but sometimes you just know, and, for me, every ounce of my being knows that she is the one for me."

"Back off the blessing request just a minute, Jon," her father said tersely. "Why don't you first tell me something about youself. Let's start with a basic question. Do you have a job?"

"Sir, my name is Jon David. No, I don't have a job. I'm in college now, at Georgetown. I'm in med school."

"Have you ever had a job or are you just living on a stipend from your mommy and daddy?" Jon David felt the sarcasm and tried to control his temper. He wasn't successful.

"If you mean, have I ever been gainfully employed, the answer is yes. You're a colonel, so I'll be brief. After graduating West Point and Ranger School, I rose to the rank of First Lieutenant. I was doing fine with my Army career until a grenade in Iraq relieved me of one of my legs. I was medically retired and afterward, I nearly took my life from depression. But I hauled my sorry ass out of the pit, and I'm dedicating my life for the cause of peace. I will become a pediatrician and spend the rest of my life helping impoverished children, and most likely will be as poor as a church mouse."

There was a pause on the other end.

"I'm sorry, Lieutenant, but my only child deserves better than being with some idealist who'll have her living in some Godforsaken part of the world. You don't have my blessing to marry her."

"Colonel Riley, it makes me very sad to hear that. Sir, I will marry your daughter with or without your blessing. All I can tell you is that I'll love her with all my heart for the rest of my life, and I promise you that I'll be a good and faithful husband."

"My daughter already had her heart broken, and this is a train wreck waiting to happen. I hope you'll heed my words and leave her alone."

"No sir, that won't happen. The wedding is this Sunday here in Anchorage. The only one who'll break her heart is you by not coming to the ceremony. I accept that you won't give me your blessing, but you can still come, simply because you're her father."

"It's not going to happen. We will not be part of this lunacy. You've known her for two days. Two damn days. Get real, Lieutenant."

"I'm not a lieutenant anymore, Colonel. I'm the man who'll be marrying your daughter and fathering your grandchildren. I suggest you get onboard and stop being such an ass."

The phone went dead.

"Hello? Hello?"

Sara came out to the deck. Jon David handed her the phone, looking disgusted. "What happened?" she asked nervously.

"He said 'no' and hung up on me. Colonels. They're all the same."

His attempt at lightheartedness failed. Her tears let him know she was devastated. "I'm sorry I couldn't sway your father. Maybe I could try talking to your mom a little later."

Sara frowned. "Jon David, I've always trusted my father's opinion. When I was dating my former husband, Daddy told me he wasn't the man for me. I wish I'd taken his advice. It would've saved me a lot of heartache. Regarding us, he thinks I've tossed sanity out the window. Maybe he's right. Maybe we should wait a little while and get to know each other. I'm sure my parents will love you once they meet you."

"So, all that happened back at the cabin can be dismissed with a two-minute phone call to 'Daddy'? Give me a break, Sara. Are you always so easily swayed by the opinion of others?" he said, tersely.

Sara raised her eyebrows at this. "Listen to me, Jon David. Don't think for one minute that I can't make up my mind, or that I take well to being browbeaten."

"Browbeaten by whom, your father or me?"

"You. We've just met and maybe I got caught up in the moment. It's like everyone is telling me what to do, from Jamie saying come up here, to you saying, "God demands this," to being hustled to the wedding altar. Suddenly, things seem very clear—I need time to sort things out and then decide what to do."

"What the *hell* do you mean 'being hustled to the altar?' You were the one who proposed to me, and *you* were the one who said you heard a voice booming in your head to be with me. Let's make this real simple, Sara. The wedding is off, and my agreement to marrying you is hereby rescinded." He looked at her ruefully. "No one will ever claim that I hustled them to the altar."

Jon David stormed back inside. Jamie and Penny were sitting at the kitchen table. He glared at them. "The wedding is off. I'm going for a walk to clear my head." He didn't wait for them to reply.

Outside, Sara's ire was fully engaged. She called a taxi service for a ride. She needed to leave—the sooner the better. A thought flashed in her head about cults and how they can quickly seduce you to their way of thinking. *God, maybe these people are after me. Get out of here! Now!*

She went back inside. "Jamie and Penny, thanks for your hospitality, but I have to leave. I'm sure Jon David told you the wedding is off."

"Sara," said Penny, "Jon David left to go on a walk. When he gets back, let's all talk. I'm sure it's just a little bump in the road."

"No, Penny. It's not a bump in the road. It's an enormous mistake on my part. I called a taxi, so please excuse me—I need to pack."

"Sara—" Penny started to add. Jamie cut her off.

"Penny, let's respect her decision. Sara, I'm sure all of this seems overwhelming to you right now. Once you get back to Seattle, if you ever want to talk, you know our number. I'd be happy to take you to the airport."

"Thanks, Jamie, but if you don't mind, I'll take the taxi. Besides, Jon David will need you two when he gets back. Please tell him I never wished to hurt him." She excused herself, went to her room, and quick-ly packed.

Waiting for the taxi came with the risk of encountering Jon David should he return. That was a risk too large to take. She left without say-ing goodbye to the Spells and ran with her belongings to the main road. She flagged the taxi down.

Getting into the taxi brought immediate relief, as if she had just gone through a storm and made it out alive. For Jon David Luke, the storm took a direct hit on his once peaceful life.

# 28

IT TOOK AN HOUR for Jon David to cool down before going back to the Spells' home. How Sara could change her mind so quickly puzzled him—everything had been so perfect at the cabin. He bristled at the thought of him "hustling" her. She seemed to have forgotten what occurred at the cabin. If anyone was hustled, he could make a case for it being him. She proposed, not him. As he walked to the door, he hoped she too had cooled down and maybe they could talk it over.

Inside, he found Jamie and Penny sitting silently at the table. Sara wasn't with them. He glanced outside. She wasn't on the deck.

"Sit down, Jon David, we need to talk," said Jamie.

"Is Sara downstairs? Do you mind if I talk to her first?"

Penny frowned. "Sara called a taxi and left for the airport. She's flying back to Seattle."

"What?" he gasped. "Jamie, would you run me to the airport so I can talk to her?"

"I will not. That young lady needs time to sort things out. Any more talk will destroy anything you might have. Give her some time, Jon David."

"He's right," said Penny. "Just imagine what she's gone through in the last two days. It's enough to make anyone's head spin. She needs time. Just let her be."

"She accused me of hustling her to the altar. Can you imagine that? Hell, she proposed." He was pissed again. "Okay, fine. I'll leave her alone. Hopefully, she'll get back and come to her senses."

"Jon David, my boy, you have a lot to learn on the complexities of women. Do you think relationships are easy? If you do, here's a clue, they take constant care. You can buy a beautiful plant, but if you don't water it and take care of it, it will wither and die."

"So," said Penny, "you're comparing me to a plant?" She shook her head. "Jon David, what my man is saying has validity. Except women aren't the problem, men are." She smiled at her husband and hugged him.

"Alright, I'll wait for her to call. I guess I need to stay here for a while before going back to the cabin."

"You know that won't be a problem," said Penny. She got up and kissed his forehead. "Call your parents after you cool down. You don't want them to book a flight." He frowned at the thought of giving them the news.

Several days had passed without a phone call from Sara. Jon David's ire increased with each passing day. In his room, he stared at the phone, hoping it would ring. No joy. He debated calling her, picked up the phone several times, and even dialed once. But, he hung up before the connection went through. Partly, his arrogance demanded that she call him. But mostly, he didn't want to have to convince someone to be with him. If this relationship was right, she should figure that out. He thought about that notion, wondering if it was just a modified form of arrogance. *Why won't she call, damn it?*

On the fifth day, he went upstairs for breakfast. Penny had just finished making omelets. He smiled a "thank you" to her when she brought him a plate and sat down.

"Jamie, will you fly me back to the cabin today? It's obvious that she isn't going to be calling. I'm not going to let this ruin my vacation."

"Sure. If she calls and wants to talk, I'll come get you."

"Thanks." He plowed into the omelet, saying nothing more.

His first day back at the cabin didn't go as well as he hoped. Thoughts of Sara consumed him—meeting her, their first kiss, that incredible night with her. He ached to be with her.

Salmon teemed in the Tal, but catching one brought no joy. He remembered her first salmon, how elated she had been, and how she kissed him. A once familiar urge came to him. He wanted a drink. It scared him. He went back to the cabin, shaken. No way would he let his life be lost in a bottle again. He sat for a while, trying unsuccessfully to banish the thoughts of alcohol. He remembered the taste of booze and the mellow feeling that came after consuming a lot of it. He wished he could feel mellow again. "Damn it!" he shouted. He stormed out of the cabin and decided to go to the knoll to see Denali again.

Several hours later, he returned to the cabin. After a quick meal, he decided to turn in early. He cleaned up downstairs and starting climbing up to the loft. He stopped halfway up, frozen in thought. He turned around and went downstairs. There, he started arranging the chairs in a semicircle, with one chair facing the others. It was exactly how the spirits had arranged them when they came to him that night. He had a feeling they'd be back. Satisfied with what he had done, he went upstairs to bed.

He had a hard time falling asleep that night, wanting to make sure he'd be ready for the return of his friends. He mentally ran over the questions he wanted to ask. Mostly, he wanted them to talk some sense into Sara.

Like events of the past week, nothing turned out the way he wanted. At six in the morning, he cynically threw off the bed sheet, got up, and went downstairs. He was pissed again. He returned the chairs to their proper places and chomped down an apple. This was going to be a long day, he thought.

He went outside and sat on the porch. Not even the sun on his face cheered him. He saw a fishing pole and thought about getting in an early session, but beat that notion down. He had no desire to fish. Going on a hike suddenly seemed appealing. Maybe getting away from the cabin would help. An hour later, his stump began hurting, which was odd, given that it hadn't bothered him for a long time. The return of pain and the craving for a drink rattled him to the core.

He hobbled home and took a load off his feet. He rubbed his stump and silently cursed. *What the hell is going on?*

# 29

THREE DAYS LATER, Jamie returned to the cabin and was alarmed to find Jon David looking haggard and brooding. That he had no news of Sara didn't help. He pointed to a chair. "We have some talking to do."

"There's nothing to discuss,. She obviously has made her decision."

"The talk we're going to have has nothing to do with Sara. Sit down." The tone of his voice conveyed no option for dissent. Jon David frowned and sat without saying a word.

"You've had a pretty good run since meeting the spirits. Obviously, you thought they had delivered you to the land of milk and honey, where no problems would ever again be encountered. Or, if you did have a problem, you'd just call them in again to make it all right. Am I correct?"

Jon David's jaw tightened. He was going to say something, but Jamie cut him off.

"Let me guess. You got pissed when they didn't return and probably haven't gone within yourself to find the answers. All you've done is sit here for days, sulking. From the look of you, had there been a bottle in the cabin, you would've made short work of it. Hell, I bet you're experiencing pain again."

A tear rolled down Jon David's cheek. He didn't need to reply. Jamie could see he was right on the mark.

"Jon David, I too had a good run after meeting the spirits. I thought my life from that point on would be on cruise control. My wake-up call occurred when our son had a car accident at sixteen. I've never told you this before. He was in intensive care for three weeks and they thought he'd be paralyzed with permanent brain damage. I prayed as hard as I have ever prayed, but as the days went by, and no miracle occurred, I became angry. I flew back to the cabin and demanded a miracle for my son. Nothing happened. I flew home, hoping they would do their work and I'd find my son awake and smiling when I walked in. When I saw him looking the same, I lost it. I stormed out and drove to the nearest liquor store."

Jon David saw the anguish in his friend's eyes. He softened and put a hand on his. "So, what happened?"

"After getting supremely drunk, I charged up Abbott Road, lost control, and hit a tree going fifty miles-per-hour. Thank the Lord for airbags. Now, I had a totaled car, a kid in the hospital, and me sitting in a jail cell drying out. Penny nearly had a breakdown. The pain in her eyes when she came to pick me up is something I'll never forget. When we got home, I went to our backyard, got on my knees, and prayed for forgiveness. I realized then that I was powerless. I had control over nothing. The only thing I would ever have in life was faith and that God would take care of me. Whatever happened to me or those that I love were meant to serve a divine plan. With this realization came a wave of peace that swept through me. I knew that regardless of the outcome, everything would be fine."

"So, it obviously turned out okay. Your son is healthy as a horse."

Jamie wiped his eyes. "He came out of his coma two days after my accident and fully recovered. The police, knowing my situation, didn't pursue my accident. Penny was deeply affected by me sliding back to the bottle. It took her a long time to accept that it was a one-time incident. Anyway, life guarantees you nothing, Jon David. Nothing. In this life you get two things—free will and faith. If you have faith, and use it to guide you, then whatever happens is supposed to happen, and one day you'll find out how it fit into the divine plan. But, if you use your free will to run amok, then how can you shake your fist at God and say, why have you forsaken me?"

"What should I do, Jamie?"

"Young man, there you go again, wanting the easy way out. You know as well as I that I can't tell you that. Listen to the still, small voice within you—and don't expect an answer to come in a flash. Maybe you have some work to do on yourself before the answer arrives."

Jon David frowned at what Jamie said.

"It seemed so right being with Sara. Why did she so easily throw it away?"

"Jon David, a blind man could see how deeply hurt she was by her former marriage. Broken hearts have a hard time trusting again. If you believe she is the one for you, give her time. You, being you, can be as subtle as a freight train. She doesn't need you telling her with vigor how right you are for each other. I suggest you talk to Penny to get her perspective on things."

Jon David nodded.

"You're flying back with me. Being here right now isn't what you need. After we land, let's get some steaks and have a barbeque tonight. You look like you could use a good meal and advice from my lady."

Jon David smiled at his remark. "You're a wise man, sir. Thank you for being my friend."

"You and I are linked together, young man. For some reason, we're on the same path. I just started down the path ahead of you. Maybe someday, someone twenty years younger than you will be on our path. Mentor him or her is all I ask. I pray each day for peace, so maybe you'll be the last of us."

"Amen to that. You want me to catch a fish or two for Penny since we're here?"

"*You* catch a fish? How about we make a small wager as to who can land the first fish."

Jon David smiled. "Prepare to be embarrassed."

# 30

THE FIRST DAYS back home went well for Sara. Returning to her routine brought order to her world. She mentally told the chattering monkeys in her head that the first one talking about Jon David Luke would be summarily shot. That worked for a while.

A week later, running in Bridle Trails State Park, she passed a couple picnicking by the side of a trail. They were kissing. She stared at them through her sunglasses as she ran by. Tears came after passing them. Not many, at first. She remembered kissing Jon David for the first time, how impulsive it was on her part. Then, when he kissed her passionately at the knoll overlooking Denali, and the night at the cabin. She didn't realize that tears were pouring until she felt wetness on her running shirt.

She got into her car, closed the door, and sobbed. *He's playing me in some way,* she thought. *What's his angle?* That he genuinely could love her wasn't even considered.

She got home, took a shower, and watched a movie on TV. As she munched on microwaved popcorn, her thoughts returned to the night at the cabin. She could still feel his arms around her, the way he kissed her, the way he made love to her. *He'll just hurt me,* her mind said suddenly. She turned off the TV and went to bed. Sleep didn't come easy.

Six weeks passed. Sara decided the easiest thing to do was drop Jon David and simply call what they'd had a "fling," or, as professionals now called it, a "friends with benefits" thing.

Monday came and she was back at work. The morning didn't go well. She had a couple of car accident victims with multiple lacerations, one with a fractured skull. Inexplicably, looking at their wounds made her nauseous. They looked like raw meat, and meat now made her queasy. While performing a routine check on a flu-stricken kid, she felt her stomach flop and had to make a mad dash to the restroom, where she lost her breakfast. In the last couple of weeks, she was losing her breakfast on a regular basis. She returned to the exam room and didn't last a minute before throwing up again. This time, she didn't make it to the restroom. She apologized to her patient and went home.

The next two days were extreme. She had intractable vomiting, occurring so frequently that she couldn't make it back to her bed before throwing up again. She stepped on the scale in her bathroom. Her bodyweight had dropped five percent. The doctor in her took over. She dialed 911 and asked for an ambulance. She was so weak that she barely made it to the front door to unlock it for the paramedics. She didn't remember the trip to the hospital or being subjected to a number of tests.

When the RN saw that she was awake, she summoned the attending physician. He walked in carrying a chart. Hello Ms. Riley, I'm Doctor Neil Martin. Are you feeling better?"

"Yes, thank you, I am. I'm a physician too. Emergency Medicine. Where am I?'

"You're at the Virginia Mason Medical Center."

She was grateful they transported her there instead of Harborview, where she worked.

"So, do you have a preliminary diagnosis?" she asked.

"I do, but you'll have to confirm a few things. My diagnosis is *hyperemesis gravidarum*, severe morning sickness. Did you know that you're pregnant? The sonogram indicates about seven or eight weeks along. My guess is that you've lost at least 5% of the total body weight. Is that true?"

Sara's eyes went wide open. She stared at the man in complete disbelief, unable to speak. She thought her missed period was due to running so much, and her feeling poorly was from her loss of appetite and maybe the flu. After this mental processing finished, she nodded at the man.

He looked at her with compassion. "It's obvious from your expression that the news of being pregnant is a surprise. Can I call your husband or partner?"

"No, there's no one. I'm not married," she almost whispered.

He nodded. Empathy showed in his expression.

"You'll need to stay here for a few days until we can get this under control. The main course of action is immediate hydration through IV access, vitamin B-6, and doxylamine. Also, ginger, taken in capsule form, seems to help. Of course, you'll need to find a good OB/GYN. I can recommend one if you'd like. Oh, as I'm sure you're aware, taking folic acid early in the pregnancy is now highly recommended."

Sara nodded. Tears poured down her cheeks. *Pregnant. God, no, not now.*

"Doctor Riley, if you need counseling, I can arrange it," the doctor said softly.

"No. Thanks, though. I have a counselor."

He nodded. "Well, duty calls. If you need anything else, just let an RN know. You'll start feeling better soon."

"Thank you. Would you mind closing the curtain when you leave?"

He touched her hand and nodded. She noted how differently the curtain sounded when you're the patient rather than the doctor. She buried her face in her pillow and cried.

# 31

SARA WAS DISCHARGED five days later. She felt better physically, but mentally, she was a disaster. There was no way a baby would fit in her life. She was a physician, an Air Force officer, and...*single.* She thought about calling Jon David, but quickly dismissed the notion. He might demand that she have it and use the child as an excuse to be in her life. No, he would never know. *God, how could I have been so stupid not to have taken precautions?*

Her thoughts shifted to something darker. *I could get an abortion. It's the easy way out of this mess.* She had no business being a mother. Motherhood was for someone happily married. *Maybe I should call Mom. Moms know what to do.* She nixed the thought. She knew her parents would demand her having their grandchild. Another thought stormed into her awareness. *I'm over thirty with a heart incapable of trusting another. I'll likely die alone and lonely. At least if I have this baby, I might have someone who'll love me.*

She made an appointment to see her counselor. When the day came to see her, Sara nervously walked into her office.

"Hello Sara, it's been a while since we last talked. From my notes, you wanted to discuss a dream you were having about a lieutenant you cared for in Iraq."

"That's no longer a problem. I'm not having that dream anymore. There's something more pressing to discuss. I'm pregnant." She barely got the sentence out before breaking into tears.

"Uh, oh. May I assume this isn't good news?"

Sara nodded.

"Let me guess. You're here today to decide about keeping the child or not."

"Yes."

"Sara, I simply cannot offer you advice on this. I want you to know that I'm pro-life. But, I'll listen to whatever you have to say. Or, if you prefer, you can find another counselor."

"No, it's okay. Can we just talk about it some? I haven't decided what to do."

"Let's back up a second. Tell me first about the man."

Her request mortified Sara, bringing more tears. She told the counselor about tracking the lieutenant down, flying to Alaska to meet him, what had happened, and how she'd left in a huff.

"Well, Sara, I have to tell you, I've never heard a story quite like that. Have you spoken to him since?"

"No, I can't risk it, especially now. If he turns out to be bad, he'll be in my life forever with this kid."

"Yes, but Sara, what if he's the real thing? You could be walking away from a lifetime of happiness?"

"I'm not going to take that risk. I've already had my heart destroyed."

The counselor frowned. "Okay, your heart will be the topic for another discussion. Right now, you have a decision to make regarding this baby. Whatever decision it is, just know it will stay with you for the rest of your life."

"How can I raise a baby as a single doctor?"

"Sara, you have much more financial resources to raise a child than the average single mom. You could easily afford an au pair or get quality daycare. The issue isn't a financial one. The issue is: do you want to be a mother? Also, instead of an abortion, you could have the child and offer it to a loving family. People are desperate to adopt and you could interview many candidates and decide who you wanted. Also, some parents who adopt are open to the birth mother having a relationship with the child."

"I couldn't bear to see my child being raised by someone else," she replied, defensively.

"So, are you telling me that you're having feelings for this child?"

"Yes."

"Would your parents be willing to play an active role in the up-bringing of your child?"

"They live on the other coast."

"That's not what I asked. You're a doctor, with skills that are highly marketable. If you moved near your parents, would they want to be part of your child's life?"

"Yes. Mom would be thrilled to have a grandchild. I'm an only child, so this would be their one shot at being grandparents." As the sentence came out, Sara almost gasped at the enormity of what she had just said. If she didn't have this child, she would be stealing a precious gift from her parents. And here, maybe, was her answer.

She looked her counselor straight in the eye. "I want you to tell me something with brutal honesty. Okay?"

The counselor nodded in agreement.

"Do you think I would make a good mom?"

"Yes, Sara, I do. I think you would make a very good mom. I think you'll regret for the rest of your days not having this child. Forgive me, but children are blessings from God. Sara, don't say no to this. I'm sorry, but my personal beliefs are now coming in."

"I know, and I don't mind. You've given me a lot to think about."

Sara hugged her when she left. She drove home, dialed her parents, and told them she was pregnant. Predictably, they didn't take the news well. Her father wanted to fly to Alaska and shoot that damn former lieutenant. Her mom quickly got over the shock of the news. She was going to be a grandmother. For the next several days, she was walking on air. Her daughter finally came through. It would take Sara's dad a month more to accept the news and get over his anger. But, in the end, he got excited about becoming a grandpa, especially if it was a boy. He could share his love of sailing with the little guy. For that matter, hell, he could show his granddaughter how to sail as well, he admitted to himself.

Sara didn't tell them about the counselor's suggestion to move home. She'd have to think about that some more. She allowed herself, just a bit, to consider what life would be like as a working mother. It was still a scary subject. As the months passed, her morning sickness subsided and she focused on doing all the right things to ensure the health of her child. She didn't want to know the sex of the child, preferring to be surprised in the end. The way this kid kicked, however, she was sure the Seattle Seahawks would have a future punter. She thought about Jon David on occasion, but quickly beat down the thoughts of him. Despite her counselor's urgings, she refused to discuss him and why she believed she couldn't love again. Besides, her new child would take all the love she had to give.

# 32

*Christmas break...*

JON DAVID WEARILY completed his pathology final, glad the test was over. He thought he had done okay on it and his other exams, at least good enough not to flunk out. Right now, that was good enough for him. He was off now and didn't have to be back until the third day of January. He gave some thought to visiting his parents for the holidays, but he didn't feel festive. He sighed as he left the building. His apartment was over a mile away. It wasn't cold today, but the overcast skies made everything gloomy. As he walked down the sidewalk, thoughts of Sara entered his mind. To this day, he couldn't comprehend why she never called him back. The relationship obviously meant more to him than it ever did to her. His fists clenched as he walked. Anger welled up.

He'd done okay since being back at school, but it was hard to focus when his thoughts were always on Sara. He remembered every detail about the time with her at the cabin, and replayed it constantly in his mind.

Although Jamie had given him a pretty good tune-up on the realities of life when he was last in Alaska, lately, he had more or less given up on meditating or praying. He simply didn't have the time for both that and medical school. But, he knew that was a lie. His faith once more was wavering.

Jon David turned left at the intersection. He was about halfway home. This part of the trip brought him by an assortment of businesses, mostly pawn shops and liquor stores. He replayed the part about Sara saying that no one had made love to her like he did. The anger inside him reached a new high. He stopped walking. Something caught his eye. It was a bottle—his favorite brand of whiskey. Through the window of the liquor store, he stared at it like it was a long, lost friend. He walked in. The shop owner smiled, but didn't say anything. He was talking to an elderly customer, who had his coat off. It looked like the guy had been there for a while. Jon David walked over to the whiskey display. He stared at the bottle again, long and hard. He touched it hesitantly, then shook his head 'no,' and began to walk away. He stopped, turned around, and returned to the bottle. He picked it up and went to the checkout counter. The old man moved back a bit to allow him to put the bottle on the counter. He had a Marine Corps tattoo on his forearm. It was faded and looked ancient. Jon David reached for his wallet.

"I've been watching you for a while," said the old man. "I've lived long enough to know when somebody is having a huge debate going on in their head."

"Yeah, maybe so." Jon David turned to the shop owner. "How much do I owe you?"

"It's not for sale," said the old guy. "Nothing in this store is for sale to you. Tell him, Al."

The owner looked at the old man, and then Jon David. "He's right. Nothing in this store is for sale to you."

Jon David looked at the man. "Excuse me, I'm not sure I heard you right. Did you say nothing's for sale in here?"

"You heard him loud and clear, son," said the old man. "From the way you're favoring that leg, I'm guessing it's a peg. Correct?"

Jon David's ire was quickly rising, but the comment on this leg deflected his anger. He nodded in reply to the question.

"What branch of the service were you in?"

"Army. I was a Ranger."

He held out a hand. "My name is Sam Warren. USMC, retired. Al is retired Air Force."

Jon David shook the old man's hand. "I'm Jon David Luke." He shook Al's hand too.

"Mr. Luke," said Sam, "we need to talk."

"Sir, it's not necessary. It was a stupid thing I just did and I'm glad you called me on it. I'll be alright. Really, I will."

Al spoke up. "Mr. Ranger, pull your head out of your ass and talk to Sam. He's an alcohol addiction counselor. I see countless people who come through here with no chance of recovery. Believe me, you don't want to head down that road. From your hesitation in deciding to buy that bottle, I'd say you've already walked down that road some."

Jon David nodded grimly.

"By the way, were you enlisted?"

"No. I was a lieutenant. A West Point graduate."

Sam and Al rolled their eyes. "Good Lord," said Sam. "An officer. Well, son, I'm a retired Sergeant Major and a former drill instructor. We no doubt will be having a most interesting conversation."

Jon David frowned in reply.

"Come on. The weather's clearing up, so let's walk to the park. With a little cooperation, I might go easy on you."

Jon David half-smiled and turned to say goodbye to Al. Before he could speak, Al jumped in.

"You're not welcome here or in any other liquor store in this area, Mr. Jon David Luke. Is that clear?"

"Yes, sir, it is. Thank you, Al."

"You're welcome. Now, go talk to my friend." He shook Jon David's hand and said goodbye.

They reached the park in less than five minutes. Sam pointed to a concrete table with a chessboard painted on it. A few people were playing chess several tables away.

"Okay, let's cut to the chase," said Sam. "With men, it's either a woman or life in general that makes them drink. Sadly, with people your age, I've had to add the effects of war to the mix. Which of these is it with you?"

"You really do cut right to the chase." He sighed and took in a deep breath before speaking. "It's a woman. I fell for her big time. She asked me to marry her and then sprinted away when her father nixed the notion. He's never even met me but he still said no when I asked for her hand. As time has passed, I'm not sure if she was toying with me or if she was just scared that I'd break her heart like her former husband had done."

"Well, did you ever ask her?"

"No. She left the state. We haven't spoken since she left."

"Do you know where she lives? Wouldn't it be easy to get her number and call her?"

Jon David squirmed a bit. "She lives in Seattle and I have her number. Sam, she said I was hustling her to the altar. No way am I going to be accused of that."

"How long ago did this happen, Lieutenant?"

"Over seven months ago."

"Do you think that what you had with her was genuine?"

"I do. I won't get into why, but I know with all my heart that she's the one for me."

Sam nodded. "Tell me a little about yourself, but let's keep it focused on why you initially began drinking. I'm sure your drinking began long before this woman came onto the scene."

Jon David sighed. "I had my leg blown off in combat and lost several men and some kids who were tagging along with my patrol. I drank because I was in constant pain and to forget about what I had gone through."

"What made you stop?"

"A miracle. But, I don't want to get into that. Sam, just take my word for it, okay?"

"Sure. How long has it been since you've had a drink?"

"Years."

"What do you do for a living?"

"I'm in college, studying to be a doctor."

"That's a tough road. Are you doing okay in school?"

"Yes. I'm in my second year of med school."

"Well, from what you've said, I have to agree that the only thing driving you back to the bottle is love."

Jon David nodded.

"Lieutenant, forgive me, but you're behaving as if stupidity was a virtue."

"What do you mean?"

"From my humble perspective, not talking to her is a slam-dunk case of letting your pride get in the way. If it's 'genuine' as you say, what the hell is wrong with you? Hell, you're a former soldier. Your first assault on her heart was rebuffed. Regroup, reform, and figure out a way to capture her heart. Lieutenant, I guarantee the way to her heart won't be found in a bottle. You've got a lot of work ahead of you, soldier-boy. Al was right. Pull your head out of your ass."

Jon David winced at his words. He thought a few moments before replying. "Damn it, Sergeant Major, you're one hundred percent right."

The retired marine reached into his pocket and pulled out a business card. "Here's my email and phone number. Call me any time, day or night, if you need to talk. Booze isn't the answer and you damn well know it. Plus, if this woman doesn't want your affections after you approach her again, then let her go. Hell, if I had a daughter, I'd introduce you to her. Of course, my preference would be for her to marry a U.S. Marine, but, what the hell, you can't have everything."

Jon David laughed. He put the card in his pocket. "Thanks for the ass-chew, Sam. You clued me in good, especially about booze. I'll get myself squared away, and fast."

Sam shook his hand. "You're dismissed, Lieutenant. Now get out there and give 'em hell."

"Yes, sir, that's now my plan."


Jon David hurried home. He had a phone call to make. He was going to win back her heart. He tossed his coat on the couch and reached for his phone. He stopped halfway into dialing her number. *You need to do this right,* he thought, *not half ass.* He closed his eyes and began praying. *Show me the way,* he said, *show me the way.* He said it over and over.

When he opened his eyes, a thought came to him. Sara's heart went cold after she talked to her father. He had nixed the whole thing. A voice within him spoke. *The way to Sara's heart is through her father!*

Jon David went to his computer and logged on. Chance Riley was his name. They lived near Fort Meade. He went to the white pages and typed in his name and state. There were two Chance Rileys in Maryland. He wrote down the cities they lived in and looked them up. One was near Fort Meade, the other, over eighty miles away. He had his man. He wrote down the address and their phone number.

*Okay, now,* he thought, *how do I win over that nasty old colonel?*

It was getting late. He'd sleep on it.

# 33

SARA CHECKED OFF the last item on her moving checklist. She was ready to go. Her new Subaru Outback was packed for the trip to Maryland. She had decided to move two months ago and planned to surprise her parents by showing up at their door the day before Christmas. Moving to Maryland would be her gift to them. They would be near their grandchild. Since she'd had to cancel her local internet and cell phone service, she'd opted for a cheap throw-away cell phone in case there was an emergency along the way. Before cancelling her cell phone, she called her parents on Saturday morning, as she always did, and told them she wouldn't be calling them the following week because she'd be on an Air Force mission. Since she had been on so many missions before, they didn't think much about it. She took one last look at Mount Rainier before getting into her car. The Outback had a navigation system, so she was pretty sure she wouldn't get lost. Her plan was pretty easy—make her way to Denver and then take Interstate 70 all the way home.

Ten days later, Sara was near St. Louis, making good time. If she drove straight through, she could make it home in thirteen hours, but she saw no reason to push herself. A couple of overnight stays would make the trip more pleasant. Besides, it would give her more time to think. Other than demanding that she stop every hour to drain her bladder, the baby had been cooperating during the trip. She felt it kicking every now and then, especially if she had a rock station on loud. *This kid has rhythm,* she thought with a smile.

She thought a lot about Jon David as she drove, of her initial dreams of him, then tracking him down, and what had happened at the cabin. It had felt so right that night with him, yet it all fell apart just one day later. She thought about all the times she wanted to call him, and bristled at the notion of him never attempting to contact her. If he truly loved her, he would've at least tried *something* to win her heart back, even a measly phone call, for God's sake.

She thought about bolting from the Spells' home that day, feeling so elated about getting out of there. If she truly loved Jon David, why did she run? She already knew the answer to that. After what her former husband did to her, you just can't trust men. It's in their nature to break your heart…

She thought about her Air Force career. They allowed six weeks of maternity leave and she would have to pass a physical six months later. That gave her time to delay making a decision about staying in or getting out. She would wait until after the baby was born and see how she felt then. She thought about what to name the child, and wondered who he or she would resemble. Jon David was handsome, so, if it was a boy, she thought he would be handsome, too. The thought of him looking like his father made her sigh. It would be a constant reminder of what she had done. She spent two hundred miles wondering what to tell the child about its father, and couldn't come up with an answer. At least she'd have a few years to figure that out.

She contemplated a number of options, like starting a college fund and whether to rent or buy in Maryland. Renting a house with a nice back yard would be nice, she thought. And, renting gave her options. She would ask her parents to stay with her and the baby for a while. They could help her get settled with her new life, and she could sure use some parenting pointers from them. Lost in thought, the miles melted away…

# 34

JON DAVID WOKE before the alarm clock sounded, ready to get on with the day. He dreamed of meeting Sara's parents, sitting with them and making his case for loving their daughter. He would ask Colonel Riley, once more, for his daughter's hand. He dressed simply, wearing a polo shirt and jeans, and was on the road before eight.

On the way, he prayed aloud for God to give him the right words to say. Traffic was heavy, but moving, so he made good time. As he neared their home, his anxiety level rose. He knew this would be a high-stakes meeting.

At eleven, he pulled into their driveway. They lived in a nice, two-story colonial home, the kind of home that says someone successful lives here. He got out of his car, swallowed hard, and went to the front door. He paused before ringing the doorbell and closed his eyes. *"Please God,"* he quietly said. He took in a deep breath and rang the doorbell.

A few moments later, the door opened. A tough-looking man appeared and eyed Jon David. "What can I do for you?"

"Sir, my name is Jon David Luke. I talked to you last summer, asking for your daughter's hand. I'd like to speak to you again."

The expression on the man's face turned ice cold. "So, the smart ass lieutenant has the gall to show up at my door wanting to talk. Well, Lieutenant, all I have to say to you is get the hell off my property." He slammed the door in his face.

*So much for my dream,* Jon David thought. He wasn't going to let the man get off that easy. He rang the doorbell again, and again. He started banging on the door. He could hear the man ranting to someone inside. The door opened again. This time, a woman appeared. She looked at Jon David with concern. "Young man, my husband has gone to get his pistol. I suggest you leave, and do so quickly."

"Ma'am, please just let me talk to you. I love your daughter with all my heart. I was hoping that after you got to know me, you would come to understand that I'm supposed to be with her. I'm a man of integrity and my intentions are honorable. Please, will you listen to me? Please."

Colonel Riley stormed up toting a Colt M1911A1 pistol. He cocked the trigger. "Perhaps you need me to state my intentions a little more clearly." He pointed the pistol at Jon David. The muzzle was inches from his face. "Leave. Now."

Jon David didn't break his gaze into Maggie Riley's eyes. He mouthed the word *please* again to her. A tear rolled down his cheek…

"Put the gun down, Chance," Maggie said, ending the standoff. "Please come in, young man."

"Damn it, Maggie, this idiot has trouble written all over him."

She turned to her husband. "Knock it off, Chance. We will hear what he has to say and we *will* be civil to him."

He angrily uncocked the pistol. "This shouldn't take long. Get your sorry ass in here and make your case."

Jon David took a step in and impulsively hugged Maggie. "Thank you." It was all he could say before tears flowed. His sincerity touched her and she hugged him back. Even the old man could see the genuineness of Jon David's emotions.

"Come in and sit down," he said quietly.

Maggie brought him a box of tissues after he sat on their couch. Jon David thanked her and wiped his eyes.

He looked at Chance. "Sir, first of all, I want to apologize for my arrogance the last time we talked. In retrospect, if she was my only daughter, I would've said no too."

He nodded.

"I came here today because I love your daughter with all my heart. I ask that you let me tell you about me, and what happened between Sara and me. After that, whatever your decision is, I will accept it and honor it fully."

"Go on, young man, but just know that you'll have to be a master persuader to change my mind."

"I know, sir. I'll begin with telling you about my parents. My dad is a retired Army colonel, like you. He was in the infantry. He did two tours in Viet Nam, and we traveled a lot while he was on active duty. Because we moved so much, Mom was the classic stay-at-home mother and she did a great job raising me and my kid-brother, Danny. When he retired, we moved to Roanoke and I spent my teenage years there. They still live there. They're good people, sir, and they taught my brother and me to live our lives with honor and integrity.

"I always wanted to be like my father, so I applied to and was accepted at West Point. I did well there, graduating in the top ten percent of my class. Like my father, I chose infantry and went to Ranger School after graduating from the Academy. I was a good soldier, sir. At least I thought I was until I lost several of my men in Iraq."

"What happened there, Jon?" he asked.

"Sir, I've been called Jon David since I was a toddler. You're welcome to call me that." The colonel nodded okay. Jon David cleared his throat and began telling them what happened that day in Iraq. Maggie winced several times as he told the story. His tears started again when he talked about the kids who were killed. She came over, sat next to him, and put his hand in hers. Jon David told the colonel how he failed his men by being on point, instead of staying back so he could've led them better.

"After returning from Iraq, my life became a living hell. I was tormented by what I'd seen, and the only way to escape that and unrelenting pain was with painkillers and booze. When I no longer could tolerate it, I decided to end my life. I met a vet who invited me to visit him and his wife in Alaska. I decided to take my life there and make it look like an accident. Suicide would've broken my parents' hearts..."

For the next hour, Jon David continued speaking in a soft voice. He described in detail what happened at the cabin. It was still as fresh in his mind as if it had happened yesterday. He told them about the five sages with their auras and what they'd told him, and how they had just walked out the door when they were done and disappeared. He explained how they changed his mind about taking his own life, how he woke up the next morning to find his scars and shrapnel in his leg gone, and how his life had changed since then. He told them about committing his life to peace and helping children, which was why he decided to become a doctor. Even the colonel had tears in his eyes when Jon David finished. Maggie hugged him for a long time.

He then told them of how he prayed to meet someone. He told them of the dream Sara had of him, how she tracked him down, and how she came to Alaska to meet him. They were shocked to learn that she had operated on him on the way to Germany and of her subsequently traveling to the ends of the earth to meet him. She had never told them any of this. He told them about the night at the cabin, that she had proposed to him, and how eagerly he had said yes. He told them what happened after they talked to Chance that day at the Spells' house and how hurt he was when she told him she felt like he was hustling her to the altar. He then spoke of his pride, and arrogance, which kept him from calling her and his utter disappointment that she just let him go.

They sat quietly after Jon David finished.

Maggie broke the silence. "Jon David, Sara can be as hardheaded as the best of them. She and I speak of you every now and then. She's convinced you would've hurt her, just like her former husband did."

"I know, ma'am. All I can say to the two of you is that I love her so much that it hurts. I can't go two minutes without thinking of her. I will honor her for the rest of my days. I wish you could look into my soul and see the purity of my love."

Chance stood up and went to Jon David. He put a hand on his shoulder. "You have my permission to marry our daughter. I wish for you two a happy life."

Jon David cried. The emotions in him couldn't be contained. Maggie and Chance gave him the time to get it out. After the tears subsided, Maggie spoke.

"Jon David, there's something you need to know. Sara is pregnant. She's going to have your child."

"What?" Jon David gasped.

"It's true," said Maggie. "She struggled long and hard over keeping the child, and ultimately decided to have it. You'll be a father not so long from now."

"Why didn't she tell me?"

"It's all because she doesn't want to be hurt by you," Chance said.

Jon David stood up. "I'm getting on the next flight to Seattle."

"Hold on there, cowboy," said Chance. "You need to give a little more thought to just flying out and showing up at her door. As you saw when you came here, some of us Rileys don't take kindly to sorry ass lieutenants showing up at their door."

Jon David smiled. "You have a point, sir. Do you have any suggestions?"

"I do," said Maggie. "Write her an email, tell her all that's in your heart, tell her what you told us, and say you'll meet her in front of the Space Needle at ten tomorrow morning if she wants to have a life with you."

"Yes, ma'am. I can do that."

"If she doesn't show up, go to her house and drag her off to the nearest preacher," Chance said. "Do you want us to call her, first?"

"No, sir. This is something I need to do on my own. If you don't mind, I'll leave now. I have a lot to do."

"Charge!" said the former colonel.

"Good luck, Jon David," said Maggie. "And welcome to our family, premature as it is to say it."

"Thank you, ma'am. I promise once more that I'll be a good husband."

"I'm sure you will." She hugged him.

"Well, hell, I guess I should hug you too," said Chance.

Jon David hugged him hard. "Thank you, sir. From the bottom of my heart, thank you."

"You're welcome. Now, get the hell out of here and go win my daughter's affections."

"Yes, sir." With that, Jon David left, elated.

# 35

JON DAVID DROVE home, booked an evening flight to Seattle, and started his email to Sara. He poured his heart out, professing his love for her and apologizing for his weaknesses, especially his arrogance. He told her about straying from the path since they parted, how he got back on track, and more than ever, how he knew they were meant to be together. He'd gotten her father's blessing. He intended to propose to her in person, and if she saw any merit in his words, to meet him the next day at ten o'clock at the Space Needle. Satisfied he had said everything that needed to be said, he sent the email. Following that, he shut down the computer and began packing. He never saw the email coming back as undeliverable. Sara had canceled her account several days before.

The flight to Seattle was long, but uneventful. Jon David tried to sleep, but was too nervous to doze. When the plane arrived at four in the morning, he took a taxi to the Space Needle. He was way early, and decided to have coffee at a local shop to pass the time. At nine forty-five, he walked back to the Space Needle.

Jon David looked at his watch one last time. It was noon. She wasn't coming. He was nearly in tears. He didn't have much of a backup plan, other than to follow Chance's advice of showing up at her door and making his case there. Two hours later, he arrived by taxi to her condo. Traffic in Seattle was as bad as in DC.

He rang her doorbell. A man opened the door, startling Jon David. "What's up?" he said with a smile. Jon David fought the urge to punch him in the mouth. He must be Sara's new boyfriend.

"I'm here to see Sara Riley. May I talk to her, please?" he said, tersely.

"Oh, man, she doesn't live here anymore. I just moved in last week. She sold me a lot of her furniture."

"Did she say where she was going?"

"No, she didn't. She was nice, though."

"Thanks for your time," Jon David said. He turned around and left.

*What the hell?* he thought. He got out his phone and dialed Sara's number. A computerized response said the line was no longer in service. He called the Rileys and told them what happened. They were puzzled. Chance called her on his cell while Maggie stayed on the line with Jon David. He got the same response. Maggie said she'd call Sara's work number and get back with him. A few minutes later, she called Jon David.

"Her hospital says she no longer works there. She quit two weeks ago and left her condo as the forwarding address. Maybe this has something to do with her recent Air Force mission, but she should've been back from that by now. We're worried, Jon David. This isn't like her."

"What should I do, ma'am?"

"Give me a little more time. I'll call some of her friends. Maybe they'll know what's going on."

"I'll wait for your call."

Twenty minutes later, his phone rang. It was Maggie. "I just talked to her friend and had to pry the facts loose. Apparently, she's moving here and wanted to surprise us. She plans on arriving here two days before Christmas. All I can say is that you should fly back and stay with us until she gets here. Maybe we can plan a little surprise of our own."

The news brought sudden relief to Jon David and then disappointment that he wouldn't be meeting her in Seattle. He liked the idea of surprising Sara back in Maryland. "Yes ma'am, that sounds like a good plan. I hope I can get my ticket changed to make it back in time. I'm heading to the airport now." He called a cab and waited impatiently for the half-hour it took to arrive. In rush hour traffic, he didn't arrive back at the airport until two hours later.

He caught a red-eye flight out and arrived in DC at five in the morning. He wearily drove to the Rileys, arriving in time for lunch. They had a guest room prepared for him. After downing a sandwich, Jon David went straight to bed. He was exhausted in many ways.

# 36

SARA AWOKE EARLY and enjoyed a complimentary continental breakfast offered by the motel. She was on the road by seven with a three hour drive ahead of her. Compared to how far she'd come, the final leg to her parents' home would be easy. She was excited about surprising her parents and knew they'd be thrilled about her moving back. She tried to put her thoughts into perspective during the course of this trip, but realized with a sigh that many of her questions had no answers. Sometimes, that's just the way life is, she finally concluded.

The Subaru's navigation system guided her right to her parents' door. She rang the doorbell. Her mom answered and let out a wail of joy when she saw her seriously pregnant daughter. Chance greeted his daughter heartily, doing his best to act surprised. After the hugs were dispensed, they moved to the living room. It was time for Sara to tell them of her plans.

"Mom and Daddy, I've decided to move here, so you'll get to know your grandchild. I hope you'll let me stay here until after the baby is born. After that, I'll get a place for the two of us, hopefully not far from here. I have enough resources to not work for a while, and, quite frankly, I need a break from being a doctor. Does this sound okay to you?"

"Most of it sounds just fine," said Chance. "But, I'd like to offer a few alternatives to your plan if you wouldn't mind."

Sara looked puzzled. "Daddy, if you don't want me to live here, it's okay. I can find a place nearby."

"No, it's nothing like that. You're always welcome here. I have another thought in mind. Stand up, Sara. Your mom and I have a surprise for you, too."

Sara was really puzzled now. *How could they have a surprise for me—they didn't even know I was coming?*

Maggie hugged Sara. "Close your eyes, sweetie, and promise not to peek. Okay?"

"Okay. Mom, this is becoming weird."

"Close your eyes." Sara did as instructed. She heard her dad move away.

A minute later, he returned. "Open your eyes, Sara," he said.

She opened her eyes and gasped. She was staring at Jon David Luke.

"Hello, Sara."

Sara didn't reply. She was in shock.

Chance spoke. "Your mom and I have some errands to run. We'll be back in a couple of hours. You two have a lot to discuss." Maggie came over and hugged her husband. She then kissed Jon David on the cheek, winked at Sara, and walked to the front door with Chance.

"By the way, Sara," Chance said before closing the door. "Jon David has my permission to marry you."

Sara was stunned. She was tempted to run to the safety of her parents rather than being left alone with, with…*him*. She stood frozen like a statue, not wanting to acknowledge his presence.

"I know you're shocked to be seeing me," said Jon David. "But there are words that need to be said between you and me. I'm asking you to listen to what I have to say. Please, Sara. Let's talk, okay?"

"Jon David, I have nothing to say to you. I'm sorry, but I don't feel the same for you as you do for me."

"I don't believe you, but that's okay. Sara, I'm just back from Seattle. I went there to propose to you, but that didn't quite work. So, I'm here now. Will you please just let me talk to you for a little while? After that, if you want to dismiss me, I'll leave and never bother you again."

"You're pretty good at not bothering me. Why, after all these months, do you suddenly want to talk?"

"Sit down, please. Let's talk. Please."

She sat down. He could see her clenched jaw.

"Sara, will you please look at me?"

She looked at him defiantly.

"Regardless of how this turns out, I want you to know that I love you with all my heart. Not a minute has gone by since you left without me thinking of you. My favorite pastime is staring at the phone, hoping you will call."

"The phone works both ways, you know. Not one call from you, Jon David. Not an email, not a letter. Nothing."

"I am so sorry for that. I let my pride get in the way. I was so hurt by you saying that I was hustling you to the altar that my pride demanded that you call me and apologize after you came to your senses. But, the truth is, you were right about me hustling you to the altar. I wanted so badly to be married to you that when you said no, I imploded inside. I have this huge void in me without you."

"You know, men are all the same. They smooth talk you, win your favors, and then break your heart."

"Men are not all the same. You're looking at a man who loves you, wants desperately to marry you, and will honor and respect you for the rest of my days. Sara, we're meant for each other."

"You act like everything is milk and cookies. And you whip out your spirit friends like they were a sword. Well, I'm sorry, but most of us aren't perfect like you. We don't know all the answers."

"I don't know all the answers either, Sara. And, I'm far from perfect. A few days ago I walked into a liquor store and almost bought a bottle of booze. That should tell you how far I've slipped. I haven't been right since you left. Remember the word the gold-colored sage said to me? *Be.* Well, ever since you left, it's been impossible for me to *be.* I need you, Sara. And you need me."

"I don't need anybody. I'll do just fine on my own."

"Yes, you will, there's no doubt about that. But, you have the same void in you as I do. I know you love me."

"Love doesn't come after one night, Jon David. I'm not so sure that true love even exists."

They talked for the next two hours with Jon David getting nowhere. Chance and Maggie returned. Jon David looked at him, and Chance saw the desperation in his eyes.

"Maggie, please take Lieutenant Luke out for an ice cream cone. I need to have a chat with our girl."

Without a word, Maggie took Jon David's hand and led him out the front door.

The colonel sat down.

"You know he loves you more than dirt. He came here asking to talk to me and I threw him out. When he kept banging on the door, I pointed a loaded pistol at him and it didn't sway him a bit. Your former lightweight husband would've melted on the spot. Sara, Jon David is the real deal."

"My, haven't you changed your tune regarding him? Maybe you said yes to him marrying me because you don't want your daughter to be an unwed mother. And, by the way, did you or Mom tell him I was pregnant—is that why he came to ask for your permission?"

"He came here with no clue of you being pregnant. He brought us to tears with his story, especially regarding the two of you. Dear God, you never said anything about operating on him, and later tracking him down. Sara, I'm not the most religious of men, but that man has been touched by something holy. You can't deny it."

"I don't deny it, Daddy. I experienced some of what happened to him."

"Well then, what the hell's wrong? Why won't you marry him?"

Sara broke down. "I love him so much, Daddy. He'll end up hurting me. I know it. I can't go through having my heart broken again, especially with my child to consider. I can't do it, Daddy. I can't."

He held his girl and let her cry.

"Sara, sometimes, you have to go way out on a limb to get to the fruit. You have, right here and now, the chance for love, genuine, pure, sweet love. I implore you with every ounce of my being to grab onto him and never let him go. He won't disappoint you. But, if you can't go 'all in' and love him with all your heart, then let him go. He's the type of man who needs unqualified love. It would slowly kill him if you gave him some, but not all of your heart."

"I don't know what to do, Daddy. I really don't."

"Oh, yes you do, young lady. Any fool could see how much you love each other. This is the part where you need to have faith. Have faith, Sara. Love him with all your heart and you'll be rewarded more than you can ever imagine."

She hugged her father. He held her for a long time without saying a word.


Maggie and Jon David returned a while later. He looked spent. Sara could see from his red eyes that he'd been crying. She felt an urge to comfort him.

He came to her, but didn't sit down. "Sara, I told you a long time ago that I'll wait as long as it takes for you to make up your mind. But I want you to know how much of a toll it's taken on me. I'll say goodbye now. In the future, if you see any chance for us, please let me know." He turned to Chance and Maggie. "Thank you for all you've done. It's time for me to be on my way."

Chance nodded and walked with him to the guest room to help gather his things.

"Give her time, Jon David. You need to keep the faith."

He looked at him. "Sir, I've prayed more than you'll ever know about being with your daughter. I simply can't make her love me. Regardless of the outcome between Sara and me, I promise that I'll be a good father to my child. I hope you and I can stay friends."

"We will. And, by the way, you didn't fail your men. I would've loved having you as an officer in my command. I wanted you to know that."

"Thank you, sir. I've found peace regarding what happened that day. I hope you understand why I've dedicated my life to honoring them by promoting peace and helping children ravaged by war or poverty."

"I do, and it's a noble cause."

He hugged Chance and picked up his bag. They walked back to the living room. Jon David looked at Sara before going to the front door. "Goodbye, my love. You look even more beautiful being pregnant."

She didn't respond. He smiled wanly and left.

Sara, in tears, looked at her father. His eyes met hers and he waited a few moments before speaking.

"Get your butt out there and stop him." The man had a gift for words.

She bolted for the door, threw it open, and ran out. Jon David was a hundred feet down the road.

"Wait!" she screamed, flailing her arms in the air. "Wait!"

His car lurched to a stop. He jumped out.

She started running to him. "I love you, Jon David! Don't leave. I love you."

He raced to her and wrapped his arms around her. "I love you too, more than you'll ever know. Marry me, Sara. Please marry me."

"I will. I'll give you all my heart. Never stop loving me. That's all I ask of you."

"I'll love you for rest of my days. I promise you that."

# 37

*Christmas day...*

GREG LUKE STOOD UP and lifted a glass of sparkling cider. "I propose a toast to the newlyweds. Here's to the prettiest woman and the luckiest man in the world. Sara and Jon David, may God forever bless your union. And, just so you know, Chance and I expect lots of grandkids."

"Here, here!" Chance said boisterously.

The tumultuous day was winding down with a collective feast at the Riley's home. The day before, Jon David called his parents early in the morning and told them to come at once to Maryland. They needed to bring Danny, too, because he needed a best man. After the shock of his request wore off, Joan Luke packed their Christmas dinner in an ice chest and they set out on the road for the four hour trip to Fort Meade.

Colonel Riley had been busy while they were en route. He used his connections to have the wedding held between services at the Fort Meade Post Chapel on Christmas day. He said he didn't care who performed the ceremony, as long as it was official. The lead chaplain graciously conducted the event.

Joan Luke was sitting at the kitchen table with Maggie. They were holding hands. Their children, who each had a lifetime's worth of pain and hurt, had found what every mother wants for her child—the happiness that comes through intimate love. In seeing them together, they knew the love between Jon David and Sara would be served. Chance and Greg had bonded quickly, their Army brotherhood no doubt clearing the way. They talked a little about what Jon David had been through, and raised a glass in salute to their comrades who had fallen.

Afterward, they said a prayer that their grandchildren would know only peace.

Jon David sat with his new bride, beaming. She looked radiant, as only a happy, pregnant woman can. They were leaving tomorrow for a brief honeymoon. Jon David had booked a suite at the historic Hotel Roanoke, known as *The Grand Old Lady*. He wanted to show her the area where he grew up, especially the Blue Ridge Parkway, which spans the Shenandoah and Great Smoky Mountains National Parks. Mostly, he just wanted to be with her.

Jamie and Penny Spell were thrilled when they called with the news, and extended a "perpetual" invitation for them to visit whenever they wanted.

There were endless actions needing to be taken in the weeks and months ahead, from finding a place to live, to equipping a room for their child, to adjusting to life together. They had no illusions regarding the rigors of med school and how difficult it would be for Jon David to get through it while being a husband and father as well. But, in the end, none of it mattered. They had faith and love in abundance, and that would see them through any obstacle.

# EPILOGUE

MANY YEARS LATER, a beautiful, elderly woman brought a cup of hot cocoa out from the kitchen. Her gray-haired husband stood transfixed, lost in a magnificent blazing sunset over the Alaska Range. The incredible view filled an impressive array of floor-to-ceiling windows. He had an expression on his face that she'd seen many times in the course of their forty-five-year marriage. She knew he was there again, back at that cabin on a cold night nearly a half-century ago. She put the cup on a stand next to him, quietly kissed his cheek, and returned to the kitchen to tend to cookies baking in the oven. Competition for cookies was always fierce between their children and grandchildren, so, with a smile, she decided to make an extra batch for tomorrow's Christmas reunion.

Back in the living room, the former Army lieutenant, and recently retired Doctors Without Borders pediatrician, flitted from scene to scene in a rewind of his life. All his reminiscing inevitably brought him back to the remote cabin and that winter night so long ago.

The gifts of wisdom he had received that evening were still blessing and guiding him all these years later. A tear came to his eye when he thought of the gold-hued man who had come back at the last minute to whisper that simple word into his ear. *Be.* This plain little word had forever changed his existence.

Sara, the love of his life, ended his reminiscing.

"Jon David, the cookies are ready!"

# THE SPIRITS AT THE CABIN

## GOLD

An anonymous writer wrote this wonderful description of the gold-hued man: *He was born in an obscure village, the child of a peasant woman. He grew up in still another village, where he worked in a carpenter shop till he was thirty. Then for three years he was an itinerant preacher. He never wrote a book. He never held public office. He never had a family or owned a house. He didn't go to college. He never visited a big city. He never travelled more than two hundred miles from the place where he was born. He did none of the things one usually associates with greatness. He had no credentials but himself.*

*He was only thirty-three when the tide of public opinion turned against him. His friends ran away. He was turned over to his enemies and went through the mockery of a trial. He was nailed to a cross between two thieves. While he was dying, his executioners gambled for his clothing, the only property he had on earth. When he was dead he was laid in a borrowed grave through the pity of a friend.*

*Twenty centuries have come and gone... Yet all armies that ever marched, all the navies that ever sailed, all the parliaments that ever sat, all the kings that ever reigned, all of these put together have not affected the lives of people on this earth as much as this one solitary life.*

We know the gold-hued man as Jesus Christ. In this book, words by "Gold" that are italicized are from the *World English Bible*. This fine translation of the Bible is available online at: http://ebible.org/web.

## WHITIE

From 1953 to 1981 a silver-haired woman calling herself only "Peace Pilgrim" walked more than 25,000 miles on a personal pilgrimage for peace. She vowed to *"remain a wanderer until mankind has learned the way of peace, walking until given shelter and fasting until given food."*

Born Mildred Lisette Norman (July 18, 1908–July 7, 1981), she was an American pacifist and peace activist. In 1952, she became the first woman to walk the Appalachian Trail in one season. In 1953, she adopted the name "Peace Pilgrim" and for the next twenty-eight years walked across the United States, promoting the cause of peace, and sharing her remarkable insights with all she encountered. In this book, words by Peace Pilgrim that are italicized are from a website dedicated to sharing her life and message. It's located at: www.peacepilgrim.org. I encourage you to learn more about this extraordinary woman.

## SILVER

Believed to be an older contemporary of Confucius, Chinese philosopher Lao Tzu (circa 570-490 BC) is the accepted author of the seminal Taoist work, the *Tao Te Ching*. Although little is known about his life, the significance of the *Tao Te Ching* has made Lao Tzu one of the best-known Chinese philosophers in the Western world. In this book, words by "Silver" that are italicized are from an excellent 1996 English translation of the *Tao Te Ching* by J. H. McDonald. It's located online at: http://www.wright-house.com/religions/taoism/tao-te-ching

## PURPLE

Purple is me, the author of this book. I simply could not resist being in the cabin that night.

## YELLOW

> *"Don't walk in front of me, I may not follow;*
> *Don't walk behind me, I may not lead;*
> *Walk beside me, and just be my friend."*

This quotation by Albert Camus describes what every person facing challenges desperately needs—a friend. Who is Yellow? Perhaps Yellow is you.

## ABOUT AURAS

Auras consist of subtle, mono-colored or multi-colored luminous electromagnetic radiations said to surround living bodies as a cocoon or halo. In parapsychology and spirituality, everyone is said to have an aura and the color (or colors) of the aura's electromagnetic energy field reflect a person's physical, emotional, mental and spiritual health. Here's some information on aura colors:

*Gold:* The color of this aura represents the highest dynamic spiritual energy possible in a human incarnation. Christ, Buddha, and the Dalai Lama are examples of those having this, the most beautiful of aura colors.

*Silver:* This is the color of those having a highly developed spiritual consciousness such as swamis, gurus, and mystics. The silver aura in these individuals is quite stunning as it shines, sparkles and twinkles.

*White:* Like gold and silver, white represents the highest of spiritual energies. This aural color embodies purity, truth, and cleansing—it is the color of pure Spirit and the color of angels.

*Purple:* The color purple defines warmth and transformation and is often associated with writers, poets, musicians, dancers, and idealists.

*Yellow:* This color represents those having highly developed reasoning, analysis, judgment, and other logic skills. This translates into elevated inventive and intelligence abilities.

# SUICIDE PREVENTION

*"Sometimes even to live is an act of courage."*
— Lucius Annaeus Seneca

## IF YOU ARE THINKING ABOUT SUICIDE...

No matter what problems you are struggling with, hurting or killing yourself isn't the answer. Call 1-800-273-TALK (8255) to talk to a counselor at the *National Suicide Prevention Lifeline* crisis center near you. If you are the friend of someone who is struggling, here are some classic suicide warning signs to watch out for:

- Talking about wanting to die or to kill themselves
- Looking for a way to kill themselves, such as buying a gun
- Talking about feeling hopeless or having no reason to live
- Talking about feeling trapped or in unbearable pain
- Talking about being a burden to others
- Increasing the use of alcohol or drugs
- Acting anxious or agitated; behaving recklessly
- Sleeping too little or too much
- Withdrawing or isolating themselves
- Showing rage or talking about seeking revenge
- Displaying extreme mood swings

## FOR THOSE IN THE MILITARY OR VETERANS...

Let me first say that, as a veteran myself, I thank you for your service to our country. If you are contemplating either suicide or harming yourself, I urge you to choose life. There are many caring people who are standing by, ready and willing to help you get better. Active duty service members can speak to a base or post chaplain in complete confidence. Your base also offers a variety of confidential counseling services as well. For veterans, help is a phone call away at the U.S. Department of Veterans Affairs (VA) suicide prevention hotline at 1-800-273-TALK (8255). This around-the-clock hotline is staffed by mental health professionals wanting to help you. The hotline typically receives over a hundred phone calls a day. As you can see, you are not alone. So, listen up! Get help and get well. God bless you.

# ACKNOWLEDGMENTS

Books that shine and sparkle require a team of dedicated professionals. Thanks, Wanda Oldham, for your editing talents and boundless enthusiasm. I'm also indebted to Barbara Munson for her candidness, honesty and editing prowess.

Thanks to Damonza for the cover design and Benjamin Carrancho for formatting the manuscript.

To the wonderful sages whose quotations I used in this book, you have my deep gratitude.

To my wife, Carmen, who is from Germany, I'll use your language to describe my feelings for you: *Du bist meine große Liebe* (you are my greatest love).

And lastly, special thanks to you, the reader. May the light of God shine always on your path.

# ABOUT THE AUTHOR

James Randall Miller, author of *Howling Across Bridges,* was born in Germany and has traveled and lived throughout the world. With degrees in physics and geophysics, Mr. Miller has worked as a sailor, seismologist, geophysicist, scientist, and environmental engineer. After thirty years in Alaska, he and his wife now live in Arizona.

You are welcome to contact the author by email at:
jamesmillerbooks@gmail.com
or visit his blog:
jamesmillerbooks.blogspot.com
or browse his web site:
jamesmillerbooks.com

# FINAL THOUGHTS

*Drink your tea slowly and reverently*
*as if it is the axis*
*on which the world earth revolves—*
*slowly, evenly, without*
*rushing toward the future;*
*Live the actual moment.*
*Only this moment is life.*
– Thich Nhat Hahn

*"All we are saying is give peace a chance."*
– John Lennon

www.ingramcontent.com/pod-product-compliance
Lightning Source LLC
Chambersburg PA
CBHW050943120626
46552CB00001B/345